# Zeus i

## A. F. Harrold

Zeus in Love
BOULEVARD *editions*
London 2007

BOULEVARD *editions*

is an imprint of
Erotic Review Books
formerly The *Erotic* Print Society
ER Books, 17 Harwood Road
LONDON SW6 4QP

Tel: +44 (0)20 77365800
Fax: +44 (0)20 7366330
Email: enquiries@eroticprints.org
Web: www.eroticprints.org

Erotic Review Books is a publisher of fine art, photography and fiction books and
limited editions. To find out more please visit us on the web at
www.eroticprints.org or call us for a catalogue on 08000262524 (UK only).
Overseas +44 1905727476

ISBN 978-1-904989-41-7

# A. F. HARROLD

# Zeus in Love

with illustrations by
Michael Faraday

*By all means let us touch our humble caps to*
  *La poésie pure, the epic narrative;*
*But comedy shall gets its round of claps, too.*
  *According to his powers, each shall give;*
  *Only on a varied diet can we live.*
*The pious fable and the dirty story*
*Share in the total literary glory.*

— W.H. Auden,
*A Letter To Lord Byron.*

# CONTENTS

*How Love Came To The World*

# Ouranus

## i.

I was born of that woman as she slept.
Stretching out my arms I grasped the day
and dragged myself out into the light.

Air swept around my dripping skin
and for a time all I could see was the blue:
the blue, blue, blue of sky all around me.

I reached for clouds but my hands
slid through their vapour, splitting them
and they grew angry and began to rain

and I looked down and there she was:
that woman, still sleeping, legs spread,
and her mountains heaving as she breathed

the same air as me. And I looked at her,
from valley to hill to plain and she was bare:
beautiful but dusty, empty, blank like winter.

Taking in hand that thing that stood us apart,
the singular burning bone that she lacked
above those enormous swinging seed-sacks,

I parted my legs and shot out gobs of sperm.
Flashing silvery-white they roared as they flew,
joyous that they were let loose at last,

and they landed in her gullies, on her hills,
on her stony slopes, in all her hidden places;
they fell everywhere and everywhere they fell

life blossomed. And as soon as I saw that
as soon as I saw trees breaking the soil,
as soon as I saw antelope and birds spring up,

I pumped that thing more, and harder,
and the air was filled with flying, falling seed;
with life; a pale mist turning verdant, leafy;

and she shifted, to trickle it down everywhere.

## ii.

Oh life! Do you see how it moves, how it spreads?
Never was anything so correct, and she woke,
and she looked at the forests and the flowers,

and smiling she reached up and pulled me to her;
with one hand she gripped that inflexible tool,
which was still running out its inspirational force

(where it spilled on her knuckles lichens grew
and ferns erupted, sprouting and unfurling),
and she tugged it, dragged it into her, plunged it in

and I don't know which was hotter,
that overworked but indefatigable organ
or the part of her that clamped it so tight.

So long as something hadn't been born yet,
a thought or a potential hadn't yet taken shape,
our duty seemed straightforward enough:

I surged out of myself like a fountain,
like a spring overflowing constantly into her earth,
into her deeps, endlessly filling her, and she

was the matter from which everything sprang:
her dust, her clay, her dreams shifted their limbs,
stretched out their stems, their leaves, their hands,

opened their eyes, yawned their mouths,
blinked in the light, ran in from the rain,
stretched and stretched and got on with living.

# The Origins

The problem with the real beginning of things is that those who were there at the time don't tend to talk too much and those that like to talk about it weren't actually there. You can go out in the street and ask ten different people about how this all started and you'll hear ten slightly, subtly or substantially different stories. Metaphysics is rather like that.

You know that the gods are immortal, after all that's one of the things that makes them gods, surely, but you also know that they had a beginning, which means that they aren't eternal. It also suggests that they're not necessarily unchanging or infallible either.

The gods that we know are petty, personal and often imbued with too much power for their own good. For the most part they're not personifications of natural forces, not the simple explanations of the world that our far ancestors bowed to and told their children about whenever they asked difficult questions: Zeus causes the thunder and lightning, but he isn't actually thunder and lightning himself. His court tends to be a gathering of legendary characters rather than strictly mythological ones.

But the gods weren't the first generation of supra-human inhabitants of this universe, and those that came right at the beginning were more mythical, more single-minded in the concepts of themselves. But exactly who or what they were depends on who you ask about them, because you and I weren't there, and even the gods weren't there at the time, and yet somehow the stories have come down to us.

Some sources tell us that everything was Void or that everything was Chaos; that there was a River, an Ocean; that Night, Wind and Darkness all or individually played roles. According to others Eurynome, the Goddess Of All Things stepped out of Chaos and found Orphion, the great snake, and that everything follows from that union.

But if you ask Zeus, he'll tell you a different story, because he likes to talk and he believes in family. In fact we all believe in family to a greater or lesser extent, drawing our trees, reaching back into the past. He too knows his family tree, his lineage, and it is shorter by far than yours or mine, far simpler.

His father was Kronos, a titan; and **his** father was Ouranus, the Sky.

This is what Zeus believes, what he was told centuries ago in the deeps of the earth...

Chaos abounds and sailing out of Chaos, like a ship breaking through a bank of mist and becoming at first a shadow, then an outline, then detail and finally something you can call out to, can climb on and sail with, came Gaia, the Earth. As she slept through the belly of the Void she gave birth, having been born gravid herself, and from between her legs slid Ouranus, who was the Sky.

At the beginning then everything was Creation without reflection: everything was fertile and life was a natural consequence of its very existence. The very urge of the universe was to make things and Ouranus felt this urge and he stood up, gazing down at his mother, the Earth, and she lay there vacant, empty and sleeping. Without the need for thought something clicked in his brain and something jumped in his hand and looking down he saw that he held there the first penis that the universe had made. It was livid and swollen and eager and he gripped it tightly, trying to calm it, trying to pause its violent throbbing, but the tighter he gripped the stronger the urge to spend grew.

The swirling molten twist in his scrotum and in his belly took control of Ouranus, who knew no better (who knew nothing, really), and he rubbed his hand along that world-spanning member, soothing it and calming it and, as he gazed down at the curves and the narrows of Gaia, in a short time causing it to pump its divine seed out into the air.

Splash! Like the first rainfall on a new world; it fell through miles and miles to the Earth and wherever a drop of shining, silver come fell something new sprang to life. Here a puddle became a deer, there it became a lion; here it makes a forest, there a woodpecker; here hawk, there field mouse. As Gaia slept, and as her open-legged son stood above her, creation unfolded in relentless full spate.

He couldn't stop jerking that astounding organ and he couldn't withhold the spray of fertile, originating semen that covered the globe. It seeped into every hollow and across every plane of Gaia's body. Her stomach, her breasts, her thighs were awash with it. She was sticky with the backlog of life: her dreams that changed his spark into matter, that sprung shapes from her body, could hardly keep up with the demand. Where come collected in her navel seas grew, filled with fishes and whales and plants and crustaceans; where a thread of spunk dangled on the tip of her nose or from an eyelash swifts burst into cliff-side life, among ivy, bracken and mountain goats.

The world became the world you know in those few ages of untrammelled creation and then Gaia woke up.

She looked up at this man she'd made, this man who stood over her, immense cock in hand, visible through clouds and whirling, wheeling flocks of birds, and she smiled as an unspoken tingle throbbed into life between her legs. It was that ache that still persists today and even then, right at the beginning, she had an inkling of just how to sooth it. Reaching up with a hand as wide as continents she grabbed hold of Ouranus' creative tool and pulled it down and down until she could plunge its spewing, glowing tip into the cave mouth that led to her underbelly.

Then, for a time, it seemed the continual thrust into life that had gone on above ground, all across her expanses, was stilled, but deep inside her their juices were mingling and combining in the darkness and a whole new phase of creation occurred.

Besides those extremophiles that live above the molten rivers that curl beneath the Earth's crust they gave birth to monsters. Terrible things were spawned and crawled out of her. Things that Ouranus hid away, that he banished into the far, distant darkness. But then, in time, the clash of their two natures calmed down and from the first happy melding arose the race of titans, the very first sentient race to tread the surface of the Earth. (From the titans, later, came the gods by birth and the humans by construction.)

Cronus, the youngest and strongest of them looked up at his father, Ouranus, masturbating prodigiously into the air once again, and saw little besides a threat to himself. Around the world Ouranus spilt that holy seed and where it fell new life still sprang up. So long as this unfettered urge existed in the world there could be no stable kingdom for Cronus to rule, and Cronus, following the whispers of his mother and of his wife, wanted to rule something.

Using a flint-bladed sickle he reached up through the clouds and lopped off that inflationary tool, the great balls of the thing too, and offhandedly threw them aside.

(Even the blood that spilt on the ground from the stump of that mythic cock sprang into life: the three Furies raised their ugly, red-ragged heads for the first time, fuming, scowling, yapping and eager for someone to avenge).

The meat itself sank unclaimed in the sea, bubbling and foaming and spinning, surrounded by schools of newly-made fishes who swam out of either end as the last sticky dribbles of come and the last dark swirls of blood drained away. And that tool sank, sank deep into the darkness and as it sank, as the creative energy ebbed out it changed itself around and formed something new, something which rose and rose until it broke the surface in the island of foam the cock had left behind and swam ashore at Cythera. This was the birth of Aphrodite.

At this moment love appeared in the world: the single-minded creativity that had marked the early period was gone, no longer did new life spring up at a touch, no longer was a thought or a dream enough to start a new species off on its inevitable chase to extinction. The urge for creation still throbbed in Aphrodite's heart, as it had in the heart of Ouranus' cock, but the power had waned, now it was just an urge: find another like you, it said, maybe together you can make something new for the world.

Animals found themselves pairing off, gods and humans too in time, mingling their genetic materials and allowing randomness and fortune to enter into the future of forms and beings. And lust grew, the pounding of hearts and loins and the sweating palms and the swirling, nauseous butterflies in the stomach and the sleepless nights and the names written time after time on the back of your jotter or carved into your father's apple tree. All this came to the world with Aphrodite's coming ashore. It was a madness of sorts, of course, and often it caused far more pain that it placated, but, then, the universe has always been like that – awkward, inscrutable and always a surprise.

And perhaps there is a little solace, when you are snared by love and wondering how to get further in or further out, to remember that even almighty Zeus is not free from Aphrodite's whims, as great as he is, and however often he protests his magnificence. A very little solace perhaps.

# Aphrodite

Something happened under the water.

As the most fertile and productive organ in history sank,
that unrelenting progenitor, that foaming trunk,
still showing the black marks of the son's fingerprints,
still spouting viscous blood at one end,
still spurting bright seed at the other
(turning into fishes as it emerged),
as that thing sank it was somehow reduced.

What had been an unabashed creative force,
a continual thrust into life, a leg up for evolution,
a head start into things being,
simmered and wilted in the cold waters of the ocean,
until it was emptied out of its energy,
and for a time it bobbed, in the green night of the sea,
hidden by clouds, by spume, by the slick of blood.

\*

The hair that clumped around the bloody base,
where it had been hewn and torn by a knapped flint blade,
fell away into the deeps with the great twin rocks
in their rugged and enormous sack of skin,
wrinkled and swollen like an elephant.

Something watched as these prolific stones,
large as boulders and still full of plans,
sank away into the darkness,
and then this something turned to look at itself:
merely a boneless tube of flesh, an arrow shaft,
pointing this way and that, filled with direction,
filled with intention, but suddenly seedless;
and so the world began to change.

\*

This something flexed its limbs, shook its hair,
which ballooned slowly like a halo underwater,
stretched and clicked its neck,
yawned and rose great and female out of the water.

It came ashore at Cythera and looked around itself,
filled with the urge to find something like, yet unlike,
itself,
filled with this desire, that was new then in the world,
filled with a lust that, tempered and accepted, would
become love.

And things were no longer as easy as they were at the
beginning,
no longer could this something touch and see life spring,
formed and breathing and slick, from its touch,
now things became uncertain,
now both chance and the heart were involved,
the first in the meddling of genetics,
in admixtures and the racing, failing messes of gametes,
the second in everything else.

*Zeus In Love*

# Preamble

This is a story about knowing your limits, about limiting yourself. That's really what it comes down to, to put it quite simply. In a few thousand years time a man called Blake wrote 'One never knows what is enough, until one knows what is more than enough,' and of course in a limited mortal way he's right, but it's an uncomfortable truth to think that only with hindsight can you know the right thing to do. Especially if the 'more than enough' turns out to be very bad news, wiping away the chance of 'enough' forever.

Now I need to begin somewhere, and it's hard to begin somewhere when you're me. All this talk of 'limits' doesn't really apply to me, in a way, since I'm immortal and all-powerful. In this Palace here we live outside of time, or perhaps it's 'inside of all time, all the time'. It's hard to put into language the exact position in which we exist. I say 'we' because there are a bunch of us up here: gods, you know. We can do anything, go anywhere, see anything at any time, whenever we want. We're not limited by four dimensional physics in the same way people are, though we are limited all the same. There are things we cannot do, and then there are things we simply don't do, because we have manners. Of a sort. In fact, there are some round here who have no manners at all, but me, I have principles.

If you ever find yourself stuck in a Palace on a mountain peak with a bunch of all-powerful immortal folk sipping nectar and munching on ambrosia then you'll know how dull it gets. Since time doesn't pass here it always seems to be the same day going on and the same scandals and gossip and I never much liked nectar anyway. Far too sweet for my taste. God, the gods can be dreary, and I have, in my time, been the most bored of all. ('In my time'? Does that mean anything in this eternal place? No, not really, but this language business is wholly inadequate to expressing what it's like on Olympus, so just take what I say with a grain of salt when it comes to literal interpretations.)

Some people treat the mortals as entertainment, while some gods really do care. Some have favourites they've picked out – cities or heroes – and they set up little stories for them to work through. It's much more interesting than The Palace, down there. There are all these rules that must be thought about, things like gravity and thermodynamics and causality and distance and free will. By stepping down into that world we have to put on cloaks of flesh and time and for that period be human. Of course, not really be human, the divine spark never quite goes out, but suddenly you're in this cage of bone and skin and you're looking out these tiny eyes and smelling the sea with this nose and everything is so close about you.

In The Palace that sort of physicality is a mere affectation, whereas down there it's a necessity. For some of us that's a reason to remain aloof, for some of us it's a reason to get involved: the chance to dress up and be a part of the story ourselves. It's a life, I suppose, and it's never entirely in your control when you're there.

For example, I never meant to fall in love. Of course not. What did I know of love? For as long as we could remember, ever since The Palace was founded, I'd been married to Hera.

Of course I loved her, she was my sister. It was only right and fitting that we marry, to keep the throne in the family, as it were. I looked good stood beside her as she sat on it. Together we were wise and fair and everyone looked up to us, all those lesser gods. They respected us. We were impartial and beautiful, but as time passed by (there's that troubling concept in a place where it doesn't exist again, damn) and we each peered down and tried our hands on earth we each became less impartial, we learnt from the mortals, from the humans. It's strange how emotions and jealousies survived the step change back from earth to heaven, unlike the physical shells we took. But it was for the good, whatever damage it all causes in The Palace.

# Then: One

I was dressed as a traveller one day, focussing myself all the way down to just one particular hillside, trying out walking, smelling the meadow flowers. This was back near the beginning (for whatever good such a statement is: it must be admitted, my personal chronology doesn't always fit with down there. Sometimes I'd go down, meet a girl, probably fuck her, and then go down again later on and find that I'm fucking her grandmother when she was a girl. I mostly focus on this one narrow range though, in time and in space: Arcadia and Boeotia, when they were green, new and when the seas were clean and fresh). I was idly building some clouds overhead, big ones shaped like mountains, heavy with rain, when I saw her.

After an eternity of disembodied omnipotent women-spirits who could dress up in any body they chose, to see a mortal with such a face, such a frame as hers, and to know that it had come about that way through the contingent mingling of genetics, through the uneven flowing of heredity... well, it was really quite something. She held herself high as she walked along the dusty road that ran around the foot of the hill toward the city. Her back was straight, her dark hair fell just below her shoulder blades and her eyes sparkled even as they squinted against the sun. As I watched the bounce of her breasts inside her tunic I was suddenly filled with a desire to get closer to her, to look inside her from close to.

I knew enough of manners to know that leaping out at

her from nowhere would be impolite so I followed her at a
distance, drifting invisibly overhead, until I saw which house
she entered. Then, nudging time forward to evening I stepped
down to the front door and knocked.

It was answered by a handsome man of middle-age. His
beard was neatly cropped and his eyes held something of the
same life that I'd thought I'd intuited earlier on in that girl.
When I explained I was a traveller passing through this land
and when he saw night was falling he invited me in, sat me
at his table and offered me some dinner. Good old Cadmus, I
thought, even though I hadn't met him before. Good old me, I
also thought, for having suggested to humans in the first place
that travellers should always be given a bed and treated well.
That's one piece of fore-planning on my part that's certainly
paid off.

All through dinner I invented cunning tales of adventure and
kept the whole household enthralled, laughing and entirely
unaware of my true nature. Cadmus, his wife Harmonia and the
girl I'd seen earlier, their daughter Semele. She took after her
mother in figure and face, but after her father in intelligence.
He spoke calmly and not stupidly. He'd had quite a past it
turned out, had even met Zeus in the course of his adventures
apparently. That hadn't happened yet to me, but I believed
him. He seemed honest.

It was later though that the story really starts. I was lying
in my bed, as mortals tend to do during the night, and I was
listening to my body gurgle and pump away. There was just
so much business to life, I was quite astonished by it. But I
wasn't sleeping. I'd never had to do that and I didn't quite
know how it might be done, but all the same I didn't want
to just skip forward to the next morning when I might see

Semele again, over breakfast. So there I lay, under my cloak, my inner eye filled with thoughts of her, my ears filled with the noise of mortality and suddenly I was aware of the door to my room creeping open and shutting. Bare footsteps crossed the room and something sat on the bed.

I could easily have swept the darkness aside, pierced its shroud with my mighty eyes, but I had resigned myself to being mortal for the night.

'Who are you, really?' said a voice.

For a moment I wondered if it was addressed to me.

'Who are you?' it asked again, this time with a slight nervous giggle.

I knew then who it was and I wondered what the most decorous way of replying might be. I had a feeling in my gut that she shouldn't have been there, in the night, by herself, sitting on a stranger's bed. I kept quiet. Maybe, I thought, she'll think I'm asleep and go away.

'I know you're not asleep,' she said, 'I can see your eyes glowing.'

Ah, I thought, it's always hard to hide every sign of my glorious omnipotent might. It is easy to forget. I tucked the glow away as best I could.

'Me?' I replied in a soft tone, 'I'm just a traveller, young lady, passing through this city on my way to another. I'm no one really.'

'Oh,' she replied.

I got the feeling she didn't believe me, that I'd been less than convincing. I considered reaching inside her skull and erasing the last few minutes, sending her back to her own bed, when I felt her reach under my cloak. Oh, I thought. And then I thought another, oh, in a slightly longer tone of voice.

Her small hand had brushed across my thigh. Its little fingers had reached down around the curve of the thick-boned length of flesh and squeezed. She stroked the fur that grew there gently before squeezing again. It was most peculiar. The sensations coursed up nerves to my brain, and to other parts of this body. It was like a tingling and a yawning and it felt good. Her hand kept squeezing and stroking under my cloak, running up and down my thigh, sending shocks of sensation around the body.

'I got the impression,' she said evenly, as this was going on, 'That you were someone else.'

'Oh yes?' I answered distractedly.

'Yes,' she said, 'Strange as it seems, I got the feeling that you were more than you look. And to be honest you look quite a bit.'

'Oh,' I said. Again.

'There's the glow in your eyes and the golden shimmer that sometimes blushes across your skin. And when you were talking at dinner, your voice penetrated me, it made my ribs ache.'

'Oh, I'm sorry,' I stammered, 'I didn't mean to...'

'Oh no, it was a good thing.'

With a surprise I felt my cloak shift further away from my body and a second hand joined the first in the dark, but it wasn't on my thigh this time. I hadn't noticed, since I was trying so hard at the time to listen to her and to focus on the coruscating electric shocks of her kneading my thigh there, but something had happened to my penis.

When I'd first put on this body I'd just modelled it on the handsomest fellow I could see, but hadn't paid too much attention to the nitty-gritty. For example, that little fleshy, floppy tube dangling between my bronzed, broad thighs had seemed an afterthought. In fact, it had looked so silly I'd considered leaving it out, but I was determined to do the human experience properly and so, obviously, in the end I'd left it on. And now it had grown. No longer floppy it was stiff as a poker and what's more Semele had wrapped one of her little hands round it.

And it was a cold hand. And all the better for being so, because the hard rod of that thing was hot as anything. And she began to stroke it.

'I liked you,' she said, 'From the first time I saw you this afternoon.'

'Oh, you saw me this afternoon,' I squeaked as she stroked.

'Oh yes, you were up on the hill weren't you? That was you wasn't it?'

'Could've been,' I replied quietly.

'Only I didn't see you go,' she said. 'I looked up and you weren't there, then I looked up again a moment later and you were, and then another moment later you were gone again.' Her hand didn't loosen its grip or slow its rhythm. 'Only, I thought you looked dashingly handsome up there, with the clouds looming behind you...'

'Really?' I managed to gasp.

'Oh yes,' she whispered, leaning closer, 'You looked smashing.'

'Oh,' I muttered.

She had the most wonderful touch in a place I'd never been touched before. Her fingers gripped around the shaft, which remained still as she shifted the skin of the thing up and down, up and down. Oh, it went on and on, and the more she did it the brighter the glow grew. Not a real glow, but something utterly special, something impossible to pin down with science. It was a feeling of utter bliss washing over a man, centred on exactly that place she was rubbing. Imagine a sphere, or an oval of energy, that emerges tenuous as a dust cloud from her frenzied frigging of that brand new cock of mine. It emerges out into the world, some of it is lost on the air, but some of it interlaces with the body, and where the two touch, the tenuous and the corporeal, well, there numbing, flooding, unutterable joy washes over a man.

This limited body, these two plain yards of flesh were paralysed by her rhythms, hypnotised by the pleasure she was transmitting. I think she was still talking but I'd stopped listening when her spare hand had cupped hold of the swinging sack beneath the cock. Less cold this time, and she held them, squeezing ever so gently, rolling them around as my legs parted wider and her other hand kept up its steady, unceasing, unchanging Svengali strokes on that gleaming hot brand new organ of mine.

Oh, I thought to myself, I like this. I like her.

In time though she grew tired and she withdrew her hands. I heard her stretching them and rubbing them together, kneading them instead of me, in the dark.

I whimpered a little, still feeling ghostly echoes of the novel sensations she'd delivered to me shuddering throughout my body. Just as I thought they'd stopped altogether another shiver would wrinkle through some obscure part of me.

Somewhere outside I heard a cock cry and from inside I heard the door to my room close.

She hadn't even said goodbye or good morning. I wondered whether that was a good or bad omen and worried that maybe something human had crept in that I didn't understand, to upset her perhaps and in that instant I knew that something very human *had* crept in, at least into this temporary body of mine and that was love.

I lay there as the darkness leaked away and dawn raised her cheery head into the sky with my cloak raised skyward like a tent and a feeling that there must be more to this world and that I wanted to always be a part of it.

Before breakfast I vanished away, back to The Palace to ponder on what had happened and my thoughts were full of Semele. I was distracted by her for an eternity (it's always an eternity there) and I think people (gods) noticed that I was a bit off-form. In time I realised the only thing to do would be to see her again.

# Now: One

I'd swept down into the woods last night in search of something to get the great weighty affairs of Fate off my mind. Some days eternity isn't enough for it all to make sense and the only way to get rid of that tension that builds up is to slough off all the power and the wisdom and the decisions and squeeze into a physical body for a time. The strata of the human brain simply can't hold all the things I have to remember and so, for a while at least, I can act as if they don't exist.

I was a huntsman, with a bow and arrow, stalking deer in the moonlight. Not the sort of thing a true human huntsman can do, I know, but I wasn't interested in bumping into any of them, I just needed some time alone. Naturally I'd checked Artemis' schedule beforehand because I didn't fancy bumping into her either: for a start she'd know who I was by a glance; and secondly, she's a bit prim and proper and not an awful lot of fun to spend any time with.

So, I was about to loose an arrow in the direction of a particularly sprightly beast when I heard a pair of voices arguing nearby. I was distracted, glanced to one side and the hind fled before I turned back. It was probably for the best, you never know who those good-looking animals belong to, or who's gone and turned whom into what. The complaints can sometimes be endless, as if The Palace weren't a headache enough of a place as it were, without constant demand for apologies.

I lowered the bow and let the arrow fall to the ground. They dissolved quickly into the thought-stuff I'd built them from leaving a faint coil of smoke on the forest floor. Peering around the bole of a tree I saw two humans. Two young people lost in the woods. Or so I thought.

As I listened closer to them what had at first sounded like arguing now sounded much friendlier. There was a fire and a pair of horses tethered to a tree and it seemed a most civilised little campsite. Sat beside the fire, warming themselves in the still warm night, were a young chap, Athenian from his accent, and a young woman, also Athenian from hers. I didn't spend very long listening to their conversation (you see, I do have manners) so I never did find out what sent them travelling across the land so far from home.

As they laughed and joked together I tried a sly trick and fiddled with the fellow's brain.

'I need to go have a piss,' he said, standing up.

She watched him leave the fireside as he wandered toward the tree I was hidden behind. There was a wistful look in her eye, or it might've been the reflection of swirling embers in the air, but as I lulled him into unconsciousness in the dark I filled myself up with longing for that look of hers. I desired it to be flicked in my direction, for it to linger on my body. Although, to be honest, my body, by now, had become his body. I'd quickly studied him and made myself into a perfect replica.

To keep the illusion steady I peed voluminously up against the trunk of the tree and walked back to her, shaking off the last few drops of golden godly piss.

'Oh, hello,' she said, as if I'd been away from her forever and were coming back a stranger to her arms.

'Hello,' I said, in imitation of a coy sweet human lover.

She patted the cloak beside her, which was laid out as a blanket, as if she expected me to come and sit back down beside her, but I held my hand out to her instead and she took it and pulled herself up to her feet.

Close to I wouldn't say she was beautiful, I've seen real beauty in my time, I've loved real beauty, and this wasn't it, but she had character enough to carry herself well. Big eyes and a dark mouth and a sharp nose, her hair neatly stacked away at the back of her head and her tiny hand in mine was the colour of wheat, though I reminded myself that human eyes wouldn't be able to tell that in this light.

The moon spread silver light across the forest, which mingled with the orange flicker of the fire and caused the shadows to skitter hurriedly and strangely across her face.

Now we stood facing one another, she stood half a head shorter than me. I bent down and bit her neck. With one hand I clasped her body to mine and nuzzled into that soft shallow skin that covered her throat so simply. In there veins and arteries throbbed and I felt her swallow instinctively with surprise.

'Oh,' she said, 'What are you do...'

I licked up to her earlobe in one wet stroke and nibbled it between these tiny gentle teeth I'd inherited. She left her question hanging in the air. I wondered for a moment as I licked my way around her ear, biting the outer edge, tongue-flickering in-between the auricle and her hairline, I wondered whether I hadn't perhaps misjudged their relationship these two. Perhaps what I had taken to be runaway lovers were in fact something else, but I let the question fall as I run my hand down her back, shucking aside her tunic and her bindings.

She stood quite still, suddenly naked, still unsure, in the firelight and moonlight. Her hands hung by her sides and I laced a pathway of kisses across her brow, across to the right side of face and down to her cheek. I could feel her breath on my neck and I bent to lead this strolling play of kisses down across her face, along her jaw, until they finally settled on her lips.

Her eyes were closed, but her lips opened as my lips touched them. I felt the air move between them, between us, as I tapped her with my tongue. Her mouth opened wider, I could sense her tongue passing her lips, thrusting out toward me and I stepped back.

A fortuitous shaft of moonlight suddenly illuminated her, where she stood. Naked and brightly lit she opened her eyes, but I had stepped into shade and the moon dazzled her eyes.

Her breasts were small, like snug fruits, and her flat belly was pale above the dark triangle that twisted and writhed in her lap. Her hips were narrow and with a subtle twist of the universe I was stood behind her, holding them in my hands.

In that moment I'd stripped too and now I nuzzled my half-hard copy of a cock in between her pale buttocks, just as I nuzzled my teeth and tongue into the nape of her neck.

She moaned a little. It seemed language had been bypassed and as I bit that soft nape, nicking up under her hairnet, I lifted her in my hands so that her feet left the ground and I leaned back a little. Just a few degrees and her weight was resting on me. On my chest, in my hands, on my groin. I hardened further.

She fluttered like a bird in flight for the first time, weightless and full of it. Oh, she chuckled and sighed as I bit her neck and her shoulder. Planting kisses that grew and budded beneath the skin in shivering blooms of passion. She wriggled in my arms like a pigeon trapped in a snare, like a trout on the claw of a bear.

'Put me down,' she giggled.

Just because I wanted to I did so, but I didn't let her turn around, although she tried to. I stayed behind her, holding her to me, one hand squashing her tiny breasts, the other covering her hairy cunt, pulling her against the growth of my penis, still wedged neatly and happily in the valley of her arse. She arched her head around, trying to face me, trying to kiss me. She sighed and stretched and I let her lips graze mine. For a moment our tongues touched tips. I crushed her to me, kissed her violently. Lifted her again. Set her down.

A palm full of black hair. Ticklish, warm, snug as a mouse in its nest. My fingers flicked and opened her thighs, spread her thighs apart in one flick and held her there. A finger either side of her lips, holding her up. I let go of her breasts, ran that hand down to her stomach, stretched it out across the flatness, the whiteness, lifted her as I bent back. This mortal cock nodded hello to me from between her legs, there where its little head popped into view. I looked down at it, such a beautiful thing, such a strange invention.

Holding her up with one hand I let my other hand slide down from her belly and sliding across her slit, which would have glinted in the moonlight had anyone been looking from the right direction, it took hold of this lovely penis I'd borrowed. I pulled it up, held it against her spread cunt, moistened the shaft with her juice. I ran it along her, moving her rather than it so that she could feel its size, how far there was to run, from her arse to her clit. She sighed, turned, kissed me again. Her hands held mine, touched her thighs, opened herself.

'Oh, oh,' she said.

Modelling the world to make it just so, I leant back and felt the air support me on the diagonal. With one hand each we guided this hard shaft inside her, just let her slide down onto it at her own speed, her own pace. The submersion was intense. A mortal body channels these feelings down such limited pathways to the brain, the buzz is sometimes intolerable. She surrounded this borrowed flesh beautifully. She kissed me, holding my head in one hand and covering her cunt with the other.

Gravity slid her down the cock and I used my hands and her thighs to pull her back up again. Almost so that the tip popped out, but never quite, I lifted her up and let her slide down time and again. Each penetration caused her to puff a little yelp into my mouth. Our tongues tussled as we fucked. She grunted. She scrunched at my hair, pulled at it, held it tight, bit my lip.

Her other hand concentrated on doubling the feeling between her legs. Not only did she have the physical sensations caused by its passage between those lower lips of hers, but she had the mental understanding that it was happening conveyed as the shaft rode under the palm of her hand, as her hand became slick with the juices that sprayed out with each deep thrust. Under the fingertips everything feels bigger, like teeth to the tongue.

She stopped kissing, sat up, still stuck on me. For a moment she looked as if she might be about to question the practical physics of the thing, perhaps ask how a man can lie at forty-five degrees with nothing supporting his back, but she shook her head, wrapped her legs round mine tucked her feet in behind my knees and started humping herself up and down. I stood up straighter and helped her.

The smell of her was heady. Bodies give off such a stink as they sweat and fuck and buck and work. You forget that up in The Palace, it's all so perfect there. Here it's so much more interesting, so much more intoxicating. Forget about wine and opium, give me the scent of a room filled with freshly fucked out lovers, with sheets across the floor and the neighbours complaining and I'll be ready for round two quicker than you can say 'Here comes Hera.'

There in the moonlight the fire grew low. I took hold of her hips again and with my thumbs encouraged her to lean forwards, to rest her hands on the ground. Watching her hairnet bounce forwards I pulled and pushed her backside on and off this proud little prick, powered on.

It stuck her deeply, struck her deeply and she cried out. Somewhere an owl answered, the undergrowth rustled, small things fled and hid in their burrows as I continued pounding away with her. She moaned and whimpered with pleasure, she positively glowed as I felt the fire rising in my balls. The hairs there crinkled, the skin shimmered and the silver glow of orgasm began to build up. I knew it was coming, I knew I was coming and I pulled her tightly onto me, burrowed as far inside her as I could and shot this borrowed load. She shivered with sympathy at my divine orgasm, perhaps receiving a little of its over-spilling energies. I'm not mortal.

And as I came, throwing this simulacrum seed inside her, I shut my eyes, felt them roll back as the wave of electric pleasure rode out of me and muttered– 'Semele!'

Where was I? All of a sudden the world lost its glow, the woods grew cold and the woman in whom I was so deeply thrust looked over her shoulder and caught my eye.

'Who?' she said in a moment of clarity.

Who indeed, I thought.

With a nod I put her to sleep and vanished the body I'd been using into atoms, carried away on the night wind. I moved the sleeping fellow from behind the tree and laid him down on the cloak beside her, laid his cloak over them and vanished myself from the world altogether.

# Then: Two

'You look different this time,' she said when we met on that hillside for the second time.

'Do I?' I replied.

'Yes, I think so. Weren't your eyes brown before, and...' she trailed off.

'They are brown,' I said, blinking once to make the refinement.

'Yes, so I see,' she said. She stood on tiptoe to peer closer at my face. 'I could've sworn... oh, never mind.'

She was quiet for a minute or so and I couldn't think what to say to her. There we were stood in the sunlight, her hair loose as she seemed to prefer wearing it, her eyes sparkling and her mouth crinkled into a heart-stopping smile. She played with a piece of ribbon between her fingers as if she were nervous. As if she were nervous!

I could feel an uncoiling beneath my tunic as her smile, her glance stoked unthought of fires in my loins. I never knew such feelings existed, let alone how easily they might be sparked into life. I could feel the blood rushing through this body, both to that swelling thing down there and to my cheeks. I bubbled and boiled with embarrassment as I blushed.

'Shall we sit down,' I said, gesturing to the slope of the grassy hill.

'Yes, why not,' she answered with a grin.

I swept my cloak out and we sat down. The sun was warm on our backs.

'Where did you go to?' she said, 'You just seemed to vanish. Father was most upset you left without his gift.'

'Oh, I'm most sorry. I had an early start,' I lied, 'I had to be on my way.'

She looked at me without saying anything.

'I'm a traveller you see,' I added.

'I don't know,' she said, after a moment, 'You seem so... well, different to the rest of the men I meet. You're not made of the same stuff as my father, or my uncles. There's something odd about you.'

'Odd?' I asked.

'Oh yes, but I like it,' she laughed. 'Who are you?'

'Just a traveller.'

'Yes,' she answered softly, perhaps believing me, perhaps not, and then she added in an undertone, 'Just passing through...' I couldn't tell if it was a question of a statement because as the words came to their conclusion she leant over and placed her lips on mine, just for a moment.

A vast surge of blood swirled around this body with her kiss, and it felt as if this little heart I'd made were about to give up, it beat so hard. As if it were making one final push before collapsing.

Such a simple thing, a kiss, and yet such magic is involved. Her mouth was warm and open, her breath was sweet and cool as it played around inside my mouth. I'd never felt anything quite like it, there's nothing to match it in The Palace.

She laid a hand on my chest and pushed me back against the grass as she kissed me again. I submitted to her push.

Her mouth, so small beside mine, kissed my lips a hundred times, laying down a patchwork of kisses before flicking her tongue between them. She held my head between her hands and kneeling leant over me, turning my face this way and that as she rained kisses across me. Oh, she had such a delicate touch, such a feel for what was meet and fitting. I closed my eyes at the drowsy-making sensations and watched from outside.

The blood had left my cheeks, the blush had seeped away and it seemed all that heat had collected at the other end of my body because the lap of my tunic was raised high in the air again by that priapic human cock of mine.

Semele stopped kissing and sat up, staring at it. I opened one eye.

'My, my,' she said.

The look on her face as she contemplated this covered up cock was so beautiful I felt I might melt with love for her then and there. My heart writhed, my lungs fluttered. My brain was dizzy with it all. Her eyes glistened with longing and her mouth half-opened, a fractional slit of expectation as a blush flushed across her cheeks and neck. She flicked her hair behind her ear with one slim, cool hand and she turned to look me in the eyes.

'Excuse me a moment,' she said, as she reached down and tugged up my clothes, revealing the iron hard prick to the world. Cool air swirled around it and I imagined for a moment that steam came off it. 'Oh my,' she sighed.

'Oh my,' I sighed as she wrapped her hands around it once again.

I shut my eyes as I felt a warm sigh of breath on the bulging damp head of the thing. From outside I could see what she was doing, but from inside the sensation of not knowing what was about to happen, not knowing exactly what she was planning, was delightful. It's rare that a god like me ever gets to relax the control, usually I'm in charge of everything, but this afternoon on that Attic hillside I put the reins away and submitted to my Semele.

She cupped the head of my cock in her mouth. Not touching flesh to flesh, but leaving a layer of air nestling between us and she sighed. It was a warm delight, being held like that, being surrounded like that, but being unencumbered. Being so close to her and yet being apart. It was a tease and it was a satisfaction all in one.

But then she touched me.

With her tongue she touched the base of that shaft, in the hairy nether land where the ball-sack joins and she slid that tongue slowly and without mercy from that very root all the way to the very tip, right along the underside of the shaft, tickling the great vein that grows there. Firm, damp and utterly without mercy.

I shuddered.

She did it again, and again.

This was one of her habits, I was to learn: relentless repetition. And the cumulative effect was worse and better than anything. Each lick began before the sensations of the last had subsided and so not only sent its own thrills coursing along my cock, my spine, through my heart to my brain, but it also remember the thrill before, and then those two thrills would complement the next lick, suck or stroke with their own coruscations of excitement. And she'd keep on and on.

She could have been a god for the way she refused to tire.

So she licked and licked, slurping as saliva leaked out of her mouth. It dribbled, deliciously moist, drying in the air, cooling, chilling me. Strings of it slid down my balls, circling round, dripping between those freshly constructed buttocks.

Ah, the zephyrs earned their wage that day as they evaporated the streams of spit.

I lay supine, unable to move as she pinned me down to the earth with this one spike, and I was so happy to be like that. It was so good to find someone who was willing to let me be powerless, who didn't look to me for the answers, for the solutions; who seemed to like me not for the thunderbolts I wielded but for... well, for me.

She changed her licking to sucking, or rather added a suck to the end of her lick. As she reached the dark head of this beautiful cock of mine, she'd stroke back the skin and suck the head into her mouth – engulf it between her lips, slide her tongue across it, brush the ridge of the thing with her teeth, hold it tight, suck on it, and then... well, then she'd release it and return to her licking. And as her tongue and teeth rose slowly up that endless shaft, the anticipation of that devastating moment at the peak grew and grew and she moved slower and slower. Until, she was there again and colours flashed before my eyes and all thoughts flew from my head.

'Mmm, golden,' I thought I heard her sighed.

'Semele,' I said quietly, not meaning anything by it other than to know she was there, that she loved me the same way I loved her. Barely known, barely met, and yet so close together, so good together, so fitted together.

'My man,' she said, by way of confirmation before she returned her attention to my cock.

'Yes,' I mumbled, 'Your man.'

And then, as unexpectedly as rain must be to dumb sheep who're always watching the grass, I felt a surge build inside me. I didn't know what this was, I hadn't felt this before. It was as if I'd lingered on a precipice for so long, peering down into mist and storm belong, the sunlight playing on my shoulders, a swirl of joy, and now I'd lost my footing and found I was plummeting. There was a weightlessness in my belly, a tightening in my scrotum and a silver shiver riffled through every hair of my freshly built body.

'Oh,' Semele cried as she jumped back from my twitching thing.

With a great groan huge gobs of sperm flew out, high in the air. A shudder ran through both my body and the hillside as I came and the clouds overhead, great storm clouds that had appeared from nowhere, cracked, thundered and began to rain.

Semele, though surprised and startled, had nevertheless kept a hold of my cock in one hand even as she'd run away, and even as my come shot out she laughed and stroked and jerked the old thing. It grew tired, suddenly withered and sleepy.

She wiped the fat silvery pool of semen off her hand onto the grass, and where each gob had fallen, and where she wiped herself clean, flowers grew in the pouring rain.

'I've got to get home,' she said, still laughing and grinning, 'Are you coming?'

'No,' I replied, sitting up with the rain running down my face, 'I have to be elsewhere. I'm a traveller, you know?'

'Oh yes,' she answered with what seemed to be an unbelieving but cheeky smirk, 'I remember. When will you be back?'

'Soon,' I answered.

I meant it.

As she ran down toward the town, her cloak held over her hair to keep the rain off, I cleared away this body, composed myself and drew in the rain clouds. It should be a good day, a sunny day. Thunderstorms had no part in love, I thought.

By the time she reached her front door she was dry again and all was right with the world.

# Now: Two

In search of something to get the great weighty affairs of Fate off my mind I went for a walk in Ilium last night. It's not all dusty plains, beaches and burning cities as some would have you believe. Some of it's just as beautiful as Greece is, in its own way.

As I was drifting across the landscape my nose was caught by a scent, my eyes snared by an image and my mouth sighed with a slight sense of longing. There far below me, tending flocks on a green mountainside, was a boy just right for me. I'd been bored, not just tired with ruling, but with judging and roaring too, and I needed something to take my mind off it all.

Growing feathers on the downward swoop, weaving matter around the thought of me, I plunged at the boy as a flaming eagle. The sun was behind me and I saw him squint as the whistle of my approach caught his attention. Even as he raised his hand up to shade his lush, deep blue, sparkling eyes, my soft talons surrounded his body and I lifted him up out of his world.

I'd expected him to struggle, but he lay calmly in my grip. His hands clutched tight to my bony bird-legs and his eyes roved the glittering handsome feathers of my breast. I held him with one beady bird-eye after the other as we soared across the globe. The wind ruffled his hair so it kept flicking across his eyes, stroking his proud cheek. Inside my clenched foot-fists I could feel the strength of his ribcage, the beating of his heart: quick, but steady.

Ah!, I thought, This really is the one.

We landed on a high cliff-edged hillside somewhere nearer to Olympus and I shucked off the eagle form and stood before him as a man. Where the beard had barely begun to show on his chin, mine was deeper, darker; where the skin of his face was barely weathered, mine was tougher, harder, older; where he was dressed in a simple homespun tunic, edged with a square purple pattern, I stood proud, golden and naked.

I looked at him there, so firm, so handsome. He reminded me of me. I have been many things in my times, taken many shapes but I was always happiest in a body like his.

'Are you a god?' he said, with surprising calm.

I didn't feel there was much need to prevaricate, after all I felt in my stomach that this boy would be of lasting use to me, of lasting worth.

'Yes,' I said, not bothering to tell him which god it was that favoured him so.

He nodded that quiet head of his, throwing his thick sweet hair across his eyes and back out of the way again as he did so. He seemed to take his divine abduction in his stride, which was a pleasant change. So often there's crying and bawling and that soon grows so very dull.

I stepped up to him and laid my golden hand on his cheek, stroked his skin with the outer edge of my index finger, down to his jaw. There was barely a hair there. I slid the finger-edge along his jaw and took his chin between finger and thumb, turned his head this way and that. His eyes never left mine. He was a confident one, a cocky one. I liked that. I liked this lad.

With a hand on his shoulder I suggested that he kneel, and he did so, and almost without my needing to suggest anything else to him he took hold of that golden tool of mine that was all ready and pointing in his direction.

With a shift of the world I did away with his tunic and looked down at him from above as he contemplated his first godly penis. His shoulders were slim, though not weak, and his back curved out of my sight to where I knew the sweet-furred arcs of his buttocks waited. His dark hair flopped, shaggy as he moved his head to and fro.

At first he just held the prick in his hands and stared at it. Naturally it was bigger than his own and naturally he was a little in awe, but after that initial moment of wonder he seemed to grasp that it was, despite all that, just a cock, as fleshy and as hard as his own and just as wilful. Although the divine powers and shapes me, a mortal body, even if only assumed for a while, is still a mortal body.

He touched the damp tip of the orbs and sceptre to his lips, planted the smallest of worshipful kisses on it and then rested the hot shaft of the thing against his cheek as he nestled his nose into the curling golden hair at its base, drinking in the scent of me. He took half a dozen deep breaths before kissing his way back up the cock to the tip once more.

With one hand around my balls and the other at the foot of the shaft he opened his mouth and swallowed as much as he could of the thing. I could feel his throat constricting around the head and his teeth gripping me halfway along. His tongue writhed underneath me, tickling, stroking, exciting. If anything he simply made me harder and I put a hand on the back of his head, pulled him on, held myself in his throat until he choked and wriggled free.

Coughing and spitting he looked up at me.

'That wasn't funny,' he said angrily.

At that moment, as he showed that spark of spirit, of free will, of mortal arrogance, I knew I'd make him cry, one way or the other, before I was done with him.

Gripping his chin in my hand I opened his mouth and thrust my cock in again. He rubbed his lips over me, squirmed with his tongue as I fucked him. Spit and drool leaked out and smothered his chin, dripping off my cock, off my hand and onto the grass.

For a time I thought maybe I'd just come like that, fill the boy up with my semen, watch him drown on it. The thought was delicious. To see such a handsome boy dirtied and smeared with my come is always a delight, but I had more time than that to kill, so I pulled my cock all the way out of his mouth, let go of his chin and left him there for a moment, his mouth a hollow 'O'. He'd shut his eyes and was clearly wondering whether to open them again. Wondering, perhaps, were he to, whether he'd get an eyeful of spunk or whether I was even there anymore. Who can tell with gods? They're capricious in the extreme. That's what mortals say.

The last thread of spittle connecting my cock to his mouth snapped and swung down to tap his chest. He opened his eyes and closed his mouth. With one of his hands he went to wipe away the juice and spit from his chin, but I gestured to him not to with a slap of my prick across his cheek. There was a wet cracking noise as I hit. A corona of saliva sprayed out.

I like my boys to stay dirty, to stay wet, and I drove home the message with another hard slap of the cock.

He lowered his hand to the grass.

His eyes looked askance at me, as if he didn't know what would happen next, and of course he didn't. He wasn't in on the plan, even though he was the plan. Find a mortal as cocky and proud as this one and a god will always feel inclined to bring them down a peg or two, to discomfit them.

I kissed him.

Of all the things he might've been expecting that was probably rather low down on the list, if it had made the list at all. But I leant over and pressed my lips against his. My dry calm lips against his wet, bruised ones. I tasted my cock on him, I tasted him on him. I pushed my tongue between his unhesitating lips and stroked his teeth. His tongue met mine. Twisting round to kiss deeper I pushed him to the ground, felt him shift uncomfortably under me to get his legs out of the kneeling position and then we were lying like old lovers, making out on the lawn.

I had my hand buried in his hair, gripping him tight, holding his mouth to mine as we tussled and bit at each other. His hands were searching down my body, weaving their way through my hairy chest, palms pressed against my tight belly, eagerly searching for the prick I'd taken away from him. Ah, it's a rule of the world, that no matter how much you abuse a boy like this, the moment you take that toy away from him, oh, he'll do anything to get it back.

I slapped his hands away and pushed him so he was on his back and with a deft move, of my body, not the world, I squatted above his head. With my hands I pinned his hands to the earth, with my mind I held his legs still. Sometimes they will struggle so, even when they're enjoying it all.

I lowered myself down on his face, my balls resting on his chin, my cock waving off into space and my untouched, just-made golden arsehole spread over his mouth. He was a good boy and knew what to do. Perhaps he'd been trained over there on the mountains above Troy. I didn't care. I've never been much of one for thinking about history, about biography. Especially not when I've got a young boy tonguing my arse.

Oh, he was good, not the best, but good enough for me. His tickling circular strokes, combined with the jab up into the centre of the star were very pleasant indeed. The tickling wriggling feelings of pre-orgasmic pleasure circulated around the bloodstream of this fresh body of mine, the neurons and synapses fluttered nicely.

Letting go of his hands I took my own cock in one of mine and gently began stroking the foreskin up and down, shifting the outer layers over the immovable bronze rod that lives inside. With each stroke my balls shifted on his chin and with each breath he took, each gulping sigh, each prod and swish of the tongue they wobbled this way and that. Oh, he was pretty good at that, and I felt sure that I could cover him with my sticky silver come right then and there, but that seemed precipitous, especially since as all this was going on I had my eye on his own swollen prick which wobbled and bobbed just out of my reach right in front of me.

I stood momentarily, removing my puckered golden sphincter from his touch, before kneeling where before I'd been squatting and before he could move I plugged his mouth with my cock. I didn't really care what he did with it, I just wanted to know it was somewhere safe. Me, I leant forward to study his.

I wish I'd modelled myself on him, because it was beautiful, and maybe in future I will. It was big enough to satisfy anyone and curved up out of a thick bush of dark tangles. It was like a tall tower rising above a mysterious forest. I wondered what wizard might be at home. The dome of the crown of the head of his cock poked out through his foreskin and glistened damply, stickily, as if for some reason the young boy were excited. I mapped each vein and looked at it from all sides and loved it instantly.

Without much hesitation I licked all round that projecting smooth tip, savouring the flavour of him. Rich, tart and heady. I took him inside my mouth and sucked, applying as much pressure as I felt he could take, whilst swirling circles across the startled little eye-hole with my tongue. With one hand I started stroking him, wanking him into my mouth, jerking him angrily.

He grunted and mumbled but I couldn't make out any words, not with his mouth full of cock as it was.

As I sucked and rubbed him, shifted his balls around with my spare hand before sliding a finger into his arsehole, I slowly heaved my hips up and down over his face, gently fucking it as I brought him closer and closer to the edge of his own orgasm at the other end.

As I felt his balls shifting and his arse contracting I thought No, not yet. And shifted his chemistry to bring him back from that brink. It wasn't fair that he should get the release, when I didn't want him to. There are good things about being me, despite the endless decisions that have to be made about the world: this ability to step outside the rules from time to time being one of them.

I pulled myself off him, hearing my prick leave his mouth with an audible pop and knelt beside him.

'Come on, up you get,' I said, pulling him to a sitting position. From there it was relatively easy to get him kneeling, bent over.

'Oh, but wait,' he started to say as he realised his hands were gripping the turf of the cliff-edge, but I ignored his protestations. He was only a boy.

Getting behind him I pressed my sopping wet, slick cock-head against the tight doorway of his bowels. So tight, but he'd got me so wet that with another pop the head of this golden godly member had entered him. He grunted something, said something perhaps, but I didn't really care right then.

With slow easing in and out I dug deeper into his arse, pushing him nearer the open air. From the cliffside hill you could see for miles and miles across Arcadia. It was a beautiful view to watch as I fucked him. I knew the names of every village we could see, every town, every forest as I slowly slid in and out of his tightly pressing tunnel. He gripped so tight it was almost a pain for me, but I didn't care too much about my own pleasure at that moment, because I was listening to his moans and watching the view.

Oh, he cried a bit then, I can tell you. There being fucked above a deadly drop. That's the sort of thing that can really play games with a mortal mind. Of course, I probably wouldn't have let him fall, or did he dare to think that if he had fallen I couldn't have caught him? Or maybe he just thought that, perhaps, I wouldn't catch him, having had my fun. The mortal mind's a mess, so many different things trying to go on in there all at once, in such a small and fleshy thing. That's what I so like about limiting myself inside one of these bodies, the brain is so small that it's hard to really think of more than one thing at once. At least that's the case when you're used to having the space of eternity in which to ponder.

I began fucking him harder, really thrusting deep into him and after a while his crying turned to whimpering which in turn turned to groaning.

I pulled out, banged our cocks together between his legs, felt his still hard, still hot young member rock against mine. I

took them both in hand and stoked them, rubbed them shaft against shaft, head against head.

Grabbing his hair I pulled him away from the stunning view of the world laid beneath us and got him facing me. I kissed him violently on the lips. Such a beautiful boy, such a handsome boy. Such excellence in all things. Oh, I had to see him, I had to keep him.

Lying down with my prick pointing skywards I instructed him to sit on it. His freshly fucked and pouting arsehole engulfed me as he eased himself down, impaled himself on my proud long cock. He leant back, his hands either side of my knees as I leant up on my elbows and stared at him.

Magnificent, I thought, as he shifted with uncomfortable pleasure on my cock. His eyes licked my face, my neck, but I couldn't concentrate on anything but that bobbing, throbbing penis that bounced with each thrust between us.

I heaved my hips to enter him deeply and as I did so that cock of his would twitch, bounce up as if it were enjoying itself. Which seemed fair enough. His balls thumped heavily against my pubic hair, against my bladder and I knew that this was the final act.

As I changed the tempo of my thrusting up into his guts, small groans and sighs became loud heaving heavy breaths. He moaned and gulped and his face was wet with tears again and I felt tears on my own cheeks.

And then with a volcanic gush I came, spurting my hot heavenly seed up into his bowels, sending it swirling all round inside his body, inside that weak mortal frame of his, and as my cock throbbed and pumped with its peristaltic motions, the waves of pleasure set off a chain reaction and that cock of his relented and he came too.

I'll not soon forget the arcs of gooey lovely semen that shot out of the boy, arcing up into the air and landing with a wet splat on my chest. Three times that cock of his squirted, jerking by itself in the air: three parallel lines of white patterned my chest. A few drops caught my chin, my cheek, mixed with the tears that were already drying there.

The boy shifted, pulled himself exhausted and aching off my wilting prick, laid on his side on the grass, godly come easing its way out of his arse, arcing down across his smooth cheeks. He was so beautiful like that, so pure and young and tender and sweet, I lay down for a moment beside him, pressed my sticky chest to his back, took him in my arms and laid my chin against his shoulder.

'Oh, Semele,' I whispered in his ear as he slid down the slipway to sleep, 'I love you.'

With a jerk I woke up. I heard myself say those words and remembered who the boy was. This was later, this was different. This was better, in so many ways. Simpler.

He hadn't heard me, so really it didn't matter.

# Then: Three

The next time I saw Semele she was at market. I smiled to her across the crowd and she slipped away from her friends and made her way over to me. We slipped down an alley, into the shade.

'Where have you been, strange traveller?' she asked.

'Oh, well...' I stuttered.

I should have prepared a story before I arrived, but I didn't want to have to lie to her. That wasn't polite, wasn't the way love should be. What I wanted more than anything was to tell her who I was, but at the same time a contradictory longing pumped in my veins, which was that she should love me just as I was, not for being the divine spirit and King of Heaven that I am. Although, of course, I understood that what I was was not the mortal body that I wanted her to love. This little flesh and blood brain I had stuck myself in was confused and it was her, I decided, who was doing the confusing.

'So...' she said as if it were a full sentence.

'Yes,' I answered as if it were an appropriate reply.

She smiled with her eyes and looked away.

'Are you going to be around for a little while, or...?'

'Oh, yes, I think I might be able to stay this time,' I said, not really knowing what I meant by that.

'Well, maybe we should meet tonight then. I've got chores to be getting on with this afternoon, but I'll be able to creep away after dark.'

'Very well,' I said.

She suggested we meet on the hill near her parents' house again and turned with a sprightly twist and stepped back into the busy market before I could even agree.

After watching her spring off like that I was overcome with longing for her. How was it, I wondered, that such a thing as a mortal could be so perfect as this? As I blinked the day turned to night and the marketplace I'd been looking at became the moon-washed hillside I'd trod several times before.

'Oh, there you are,' she said with a surprised little giggle. 'I wondered where you'd got to.'

'Ah, yes, well...'

'Oh, shush sir,' she said, 'Come and kiss me.'

I stepped up the hill to where she stood above me, silhouetted by the moon.

'Kiss me.'

I leant up and placed my lips upon hers.

She sighed contentedly as she wrapped her arms around my broad shoulders.

'I don't know what it is,' she said, sighing between kisses, 'About you that makes me this way. But, I think I love you. Which is crazy,' still between kisses, 'Because I hardly know you. I've only ever seen you a handful of times and months go by between your visits,' still whilst kissing, 'But I dream of you, I long for you. You sir, I think are the man I love. The man I've been waiting for.'

My heart beat ecstatically at this news. Without any godly tricks on my part, she loved me, just as I was. My lungs dragged deep draughts of air and my brain spun. This body I'd built blushed and I wondered whether I'd perhaps forgotten something when putting it together. But I think, I know, that it was just the over-spillage of my emotions affecting the frame.

Then she spoke again.

'But who are you?'

I told her the name I'd told her before.

'Oh, I know that, but who are you really?'

She peered into my eyes and I felt, with a shock, that she could see inside me and knew I that I was a fraud. What to say?

I said nothing and kissed her instead, but she pulled away.

'Oh, you don't want to tell me? Well,' she said, 'It doesn't matter. Not now. Not right now. But I'll find out one day, oh yes. But now... now, I'm hungry.'

As she spoke I felt her hand once again wrap itself around the meaty penis that hung thick and firm between these handsome human thighs I'd made for her.

She leant in close and kissed me, moving quickly from my mouth, across my jaw-line, down to my neck, where she bit playfully. It was strange and delightful and my prick throbbed in her little hand. She gnawed away at my neck, pushing my cloak to one side and working on my shoulder. She sent such tingling giggling sensations playing through my nerves that I laughed and couldn't help but push her away.

I looked at her in the moonlight where she stood a little way away from me. My cock bobbed out of the front of my cloak between us and we both laughed.

I fell to my knees before her. Long had I been worshipped but tonight I wanted to worship her. I pulled her to me, rested my head on her stomach. I held her close to me with an arm around her back, with a spread palm stretching to cover her flank. I listened to the insistent and interminable workings of her insides. It was amazing. To think that such limited beings as humans were still so very complicated when it came down to it.

With my other hand I traced a line of fingerprints on her thigh, running my fingertips up under the hem of her tunic, along the bare flesh, the skin, into darkness. The miracle of flesh. Ah, whoever invented it knew a trick or two about organising matter in enjoyable ways. To think, everything could have remained stone for all time, or mud. But no, certain bits of the world were transmuted into this living, motive, warm stuff. It walks about by itself, it gurgles and breathes and digests all by itself. If this isn't a marvel, I don't know what is.

I loved to find her. To discover new bits of her. I moved my head away from her stomach, leant down lower and kissed her feet. Spitting dust I kissed her ankles. I touched them, stroked them. With my fingertips I prepared each inch of her for my lips. Kissing my way up her calves, stroking her hair, laying a path of tribute, tip by tip, kiss by kiss. Oh, I rose up to her knees, kissing inside and outside, loving the front and back. She stumbled and opened her legs wider so I could explore her thighs. The moon slid behind some roving clouds.

With my fingertips I brushed their insides, and she twitched as I did so. I couldn't help but giggle with the joy of it. I like to think she was smiling, though I didn't look at her face. I ran my hands down the outsides of her thighs and then up again, to cup her buttocks. They filled my palms with cool, white flesh as if the parts were made for each other: palm and cheek. Such forethought someone had had.

As I clutched her bum I kissed up between her thighs. Alternating a ladder of kisses on each inner surface until I found my nose nestling in a nest of black hair. Oh, goodness, I thought to myself.

I heard Semele sigh above me.

I held her buttocks and shifted my legs to make myself more

comfortable underneath her. I noticed that the tip of my nose was damp.

I nuzzled upwards again, following my nose into the tangle of hair and finding that the deeper I explored the wetter my nose was getting, and the louder my dear Semele was sighing.

I could feel one of her hands on the top of my head, holding onto my hair.

I followed my nose with my tongue, parting the hairs and finding her secret garden's secret centre. Not knowing exactly what to do I licked, trying to emulate the rhythms that she had previously used on me. Just stroking along that watercourse from the back to the front, up and down, as I squeezed her buttocks and pulled her weight down onto my face.

Her fingers entwined tighter in my hair and I could feel her thighs clamping around my ears. I took these to be good signs. She'd ask me to stop, wouldn't she, if she didn't like it?

The more I licked her the wetter she seemed to be and it was hard to know whether it was my spit or her own juices that were to account for this phenomenon, although I could taste her sharp sweet musk with every stroke of the tongue.

I decided to change my approach, moving away from the repeated unidirectional stroking and tried some things a little more exploratory. I discovered the exact shape of her and dove my tongue inside her, stretching the real world a little to reach deeper. I slid my tongue up along one side of her labia and down the other, a wide circle that opened her lips wider and wider, before sliding my tongue once again up inside her, to where the flavour changes, where it becomes sharper.

Her fingers in my hair pulled me away from her spasming thighs, pulled my face from out of her secret valley. My face must have glistened in the starlight, smeared as it was with her juices.

'Oh,' she said, looking down into my eyes, 'My man. My special, secret man.'

She knelt beside me. She almost slumped beside me and leant her head on my chest.

'Oh,' she said again.

Just as I thought she might be tired, might be thinking, as mortals so often do, of sleeping, she sat up, held herself away from me at arm's length. She looked at me, with one hand on my neck, and one on my shoulder and hooked a leg over mine.

I was still knelt and now she knelt with a knee either side of me. Taking the hand off my shoulder she reached down between her legs, down to that dark downy temple she kept hidden there and with barely a touch she lowered herself onto my untouched once again newly made prick.

I felt her lips take me in hand, felt the wet hot opening of her vagina embrace the head of this mortal cock and then, like a magician she made it vanish. In fact she transmuted that cock into air: as it burrowed into her, as she sank herself down on it, she expired a sigh and a laugh so heartfelt that it was as if I were coming out of her mouth, as if I were passing straight through her. Some time before the steam engine would ever reach these shores that's what she did, took my timber, burnt it up and turned it to hot air, driving her insides, whirling the cogs and wheels and fluttering pleasures that made her so perfectly and beautifully human. Oh, she loved me so much.

Kissing me again, for the hundredth time, for the thousandth time that night (and still never losing its peculiar appeal, its unremitting novelty), she bucked up and down in my lap, twisting and churning her clutching cunt around my cock. I could feel magic building up inside it, a huge spring was being wound tighter and tighter in my stomach, in my chest. My brain was fuddled and my penis was singing to me.

'You do love me?' she asked, between kisses and between grunts.

'Yes, yes, oh, gods yes,' I answered, between kisses, sighs and distractions.

'Oh gods, I love you too,' she said as she rocked up and down.

Her arms were wrapped around my neck, our cheeks pressing together, her heavy breasts squashed against my chest, with just the soft wool of her tunic between us. My hands roved across her back, resting on her buttocks, lifting her, parting her cheeks, feeling the thrust of my cock-shaft as it slid in and out of her tightness, of her wetness.

As she bounced there in my lap, there on a hillside, with dawn threatening the horizon, as the Morning Star slid down toward her bed, she whispered in my ear fateful words. Had I known at the time where they would lead us I would have shut my ears, plugged them up with wax just as wily Odysseus would. But I didn't know. I was a fool. And a fool living in a tiny mortal body, locked off from wisdom and eternity for a short while.

'I love... you,' she said, between puffs, 'I'd do anything... for you, you know... anything for you...'

Simple enough words. The words of a lover, of a beloved. I know that. I knew that even then. But here's where the trouble starts. There I was, buried balls-deep inside her, conjoined as close as two humans can be, enjoying the moment, lost in the moment, starry-eyed, love-struck but sadly not dumb-struck.

'I love you too,' I said. 'I'd do anything for you, too,' I said. Idiot.

Thinking of that simple, little vow dropped into the conversation, into the fucking, in passing, I'm quite distracted. I could've seen the future even then, had I bothered to look. Had I wanted to look.

That evening, that morning, as dawn rose above the horizon, as day returned to Boeotia, as the cocks crowed and farmers did whatever it was that farmers do at that time of day, she came wriggling and giggling and crying and laughing in my lap, sat perched off this godly hard prick. Her muscles shivered, her legs clutched around me, she bit into my neck and I came with her. Hot glowing seed ricocheted inside her cunt, leaked out around my cock, across my balls, which were soaked with sweat and her juices and now my sperm. A lawn grew up around us before she made her way home and I vanished, leaving her with promises that I'd be passing through again soon.

I watched her walk away down the hillside and wondered how life could be better than this. Her arse swang in a way that made me feel hard again. I chuckled, smiled and vanished this body into a puff of butterflies and a slightly less interesting diffuse cloud of second-hand atoms.

# Now: Three

L ast night was interesting.

I'd been getting a bit of respite from the talking-shop that The Palace had become by treading the earth again. It's the usual story.

With the distant stars above me and the hard rock beneath me I was feeling small but free once more. Well, freer perhaps. There still nagged a worry in my mind that I couldn't quite place. The forest I was in seemed familiar, something about the phase of the moon rang a bell, but the brain of a stag is not the most capacious of structures and whatever it was that was nagging at me couldn't quite realise itself.

With a suddenness that struck me quite solid with fear there came a crashing from the undergrowth to my right. Trees shook and a rainfall of leaves and insects fluttered down in the dark.

I stood stock still in my stag form and peered into the darkness. You find in a body like this, with a tiny proud brain like this, there are two diametrically opposed reactions to the unexpected: thoughtless flight; or the dumb imagining that one can hide in full view by being motionless. Without my conscious say so I'd opted for the latter and in an instant I regretted it as from out the dark loomed the great shape of a bear reared up on its hind legs.

Now, I had antlers and I had hooves and I had a godly strength and will and had I wanted to I could have avoided those vast claws and that slavering jaw with its yellow teeth. I could've vanished or stopped the world or simply struck out in self-defence but instead I happily let the arrow that flew across my broad shoulder, skimming the fur there (I felt it tickle), slam into the bear's shaggy throat, plunging it backwards into the night. It fell heavily. Saplings broke and the ground shook. All around in the dark animals scurried, flew, cried out and finally settled down.

The bear moaned and bubbled as it choked on the blood that was filling its throat. Its huge paws clawed ineffectually at the wooden shaft that had slammed through it. I knew those arrows and there was no escaping them, no way it would ever free itself from death's clammy embrace.

Eventually the bear lay silent.

I turned around.

'Father,' said Artemis, shouldering her bow.

'Artemis,' I said, bypassing the dull vocal cords of the deer and projecting straight into the air.

'You looked like you needed help,' she said.

'No,' I answered, 'But thank you.'

I'd always thought good manners cost a soul very little and honesty is usually appreciated. She nodded back at me.

Never been much of a one for big conversations, Artemis. A strange god that one. She lives down here in the world, spending her time hunting game, running round with a gang of girls and presumably answering the odd prayer from her temples.

It's the girls that interest me. She has these followers, nymphs mostly, who hang on her every footstep, but whom she never seems to notice. All she cares for is the kill, is the hunt. Not one to interest herself with sex. But, it takes all sorts to fill this world, and that's fine with me, though if she only looked she'd see how those girls of hers are pining away with sickness for lusting after her.

I'd been wandering her woods before once, and I'd done the archetypical foolish mortal thing of stumbling upon the headquarters of her merry band. Moving silently through the world I'd pushed aside a branch and stopped. There before me, framed by the trees, highlighted in the gap I'd just made, was a waterfall, a rock pool, and Artemis stark naked washing herself.

Now, she's family, so I have to love her, that's taken as read, but I must say, being honest, that she's not exactly my type. She's skinny and scratched, muscular and bruised. Tough. She keeps her hair cut short and her breasts small. She says it's so the forest can move more easily around her. I say it's because she doesn't care enough. I mean, all it takes is a thought to resurface a mortal body, to shuck off scars and mend bruises, but she doesn't care. To her they're memories of good hunts and of the ones that got away.

Of course, under this skinny boyish body lies an Immortal heart, and you can see it shine through if you catch her at the right angle, and it's only natural that her nymphs want to bed her. I mean looking at her secretly that night from the sidelines I wanted to bed her, but there's no one, not even me, going to ever get to tumble my Artemis. She's my girl, no kidding, and she'll destroy anyone who tries to tup her, as soon as blink.

I nodded an apology for the intrusion, and backed away from that pool. Seeing who I was, even through whatever disguise I was wearing, she nodded back and let me go. But I couldn't just let it go at that. Something had risen in me, seeing her nakedness.

I slipped into her body, a simulacrum I made on the spot, and before she finished bathing I slipped into her camp, stood amongst her nymphs and handmaidens and pointed to one at random.

'Come with me,' I said, gesturing behind me into the dark wood, 'I need your help.'

Oh, you should've seen this one's eyes light up. You should've seen the rest of the eyes pour envy!

When we were out of the firelight, when we'd walked some way into the night I opened a little bower in the woods, lined it with moss and lay down in it.

This nymph I'd picked looked confused. She'd followed me silently through the woods and now stood gazing down at me with a look of utter confusion on her face.

'Callisto,' I said, clutching her name from the surface of her mind, 'I need you.'

'But...' she said.

It was clear, from what I heard in her brain, that she'd dreamt of a moment like this for so long, but that now it was here she couldn't believe it had really arrived. Of course it hadn't really arrived, but her beloved Artemis was lying there with her arms and her legs open to her, begging her to come down and fuck her. What was a nymph to do? In fact, what was a god to do, me or Artemis, with a nymph who was so frozen with fear?

Well, the only answer seemed to be to use a bit of influence. I beckoned with a crooked finger, tugged at the world between us as if it were elastic and felt her fall onto me. Sometimes one has to force the first touch, but after that it's usually easy. And it was.

The moment I convinced Callisto that I, Artemis, wasn't fooling around, she fell into the story. I wrapped my arms around her arms, across her back, lifted my legs up above her thighs, crossed my ankles over her buttocks and held her in that embrace as she wept into my neck.

She felt so warm against me, her breasts larger and fuller

and much sexier than mine squashing themselves across my chest. Her stomach rubbed against mine as I pulled her tight, wedged her tight in my grip. Her tears welled up out of her, a hundred years of silent longing suddenly given release. Her sighs heaved their way out of her, her chest shuddered and my neck grew wetter.

But in time she regained herself, apologised quietly into my hair and her sobbing changed to kissing. She lip-bit my neck. Covering me with affection. Pushing my head back to stretch my throat out to her, pale and smooth and golden, she nibbled at it, licked it, kissed it. I could feel the moistness dry immediately into the cool night breeze. The contrast between that and between the feel of her warm body against mine was delicious.

In time I unwrapped her. Laid my arms down, lowered my legs. Let her move about of her own volition. I knew she wasn't running away. I was surprised though, all the time, at how she couldn't tell I wasn't her Artemis, that I wasn't the one she loved. My copy wasn't perfect, my body wasn't identical. The noises I made were not those that that prim little murderous virgin would've made had she been kissed, licked or fucked. We all know that. There was no way at all that Callisto could not have known that, but she was so smitten, so desirous of her leader, her athletic supple huntress-nun of a god, that she pretended not to notice I wasn't her. Maybe she thought she was in a dream, maybe she thought she was sick and writhing in a feverish vision. I don't know. But she was fulfilling a wish, a fantasy and she was going to take full advantage it seemed. Possibly the one opportunity, that wasn't a silent night's daydream with her own hand on her own cunt.

I lay back as she patterned kisses on me. I kissed back when she held my face, kissed my mouth. I stroked her shoulder, her arm as she leant above me and licked my cheekbones, my eyelids. When she lowered her sweet nipple into my mouth I bit it. She pulled it away, lowered it again. I sucked it. She left it there. Then swapped it for the other. Then took them both away and kissed me again.

In the moonlight I noticed her cheeks were still damp with tears. I sat up on my elbows and kissed them away. Swapping salt water for spit. She laughed, kissed me again, laughed and cried some more. I lay back down.

She sucked first on my right nipple, gently at first, feeling it grew hard and rubbery between her lips. Then she twisted it in her mouth, licked across the plateau of its crown, its summit and then sucked it up, lifted my whole little breast between her lips by this stiff brown peak. I felt rivers of happiness circle round my body, centred on her mouth, but writhing through blood and nerve. My other tit grew itchy, uneven, my mouth opened for kisses, for her tongue, for anything, air even. And the throbbing between my legs grew.

She swapped breasts, treating my fresh virgin nipple in the same way that she'd dealt with the now well broken in one. The mirror image sensation circled me, in reverse this time, circling from the other centre.

I clutched her head, pulled her onto me, squashed her face into my tit, squeezed her into me. I felt overcome by a sudden panic that maybe she'd stop. Maybe she would work out I was duping her and she'd go away, leaving me alone for the night. I felt an insecurity I hadn't felt for eternities surge through me.

She freed herself from my grip, however, and edged up my body to kiss my mouth again. I submitted to her touch and could feel her hard nipples squashed themselves into my chest, folding in on themselves as she leant on my thin frame. The weight of her above me, though only slight (nymphs not being the heaviest of mortal creatures), was satisfying in its security. It sang that she was there, a real earthy body, that she wasn't a figment, wasn't a ghost about to drift off. I loved her for being there, for being real.

As she kissed me, as she rubbed cheek to cheek, as she squeezed one small tit and nibbled on my ear-lobe, she lowered her other hand between my thighs. Electric shocks jerked my legs apart, rocked my stomach. I muttered obscure words that even I couldn't identify. I sighed and bit her shoulder.

Her fingers found me wet. They slid across me with that frictionless ease that every pussy acquires. So wet that she wiped her fingers in my sparse pubes before flicking my clit. I think she was keeping her fingers out of the deepest pools, out of the rivers, for fear of being swept away. But she flicked my clit with no mercy. It was a hard sharp blow, not the gentle rub, not the slowly applied pressure I had expected her to use. She flicked, finger from thumb, and each time she did a sharp, painful ripple of sparks shot up from my crotch to my nipples, to my mouth.

I had been, I mean Artemis had been, for so many years a cunt-tease, I think, that Callisto was determined to take some of her frustrations out on me/her. But I didn't care. I was lying down, being adored and that was good enough for me that night. Even if it hurt it was a beautiful hurt.

She stopped kissing me. She sat up. One finger was still connected to me via my clitoris, but that was motionless. Only the threat of it kept me on edge. I shifted to give it some movement, some friction, but she was faster and moved with my movements to keep it still. Looking at me through the darkness with her supernatural eyes she traced my body with her fingernails. In an absent thought I pondered how one kept nails so neat in the forest. They were even, not long, but clean and even, and she dragged them slowly down my body.

She drew paths from my eyes, from my chin, across my shoulders, my collarbone, around my nipples, across my stomach, around my navel, pointing arrows to the swollen opening of my cunt. But she never reached it. Inches away from my parted lips she'd stop and return those hard nails to the top, start again as if, perhaps, she'd missed a line, had missed a turning, had forgotten something she needed. The frustration was exquisite. She did the same from my feet. The frustration was devastating and annoying and I couldn't do anything about it.

She pushed open my legs, held them open against my will, looked at me. As a god I'd never quite given myself so freely, not for an eternity, but this seemed right. The submission to Callisto's power was right, tonight. Tomorrow perhaps we'd do this a different way.

She traced along the lips of my spreading cunt with her fingertips. Wiped the excess juice on my thighs. She parted me. Spread me open like a butterfly. Pinned me, examined the patterns of my petals. The pink interior of me was open to her. The peeking bud of my clit waved at her. The moist, slippery tunnel sighed at her, contracted, winked at her. I watched all this, disembodied, but still in me. A good trick if you can do it. Her fingers spread my lips as she finally crouched in close and lowered her tongue to drink from me.

Like a deer leaning to drink from a forest pool, she bowed her head slowly, reverently, as if always keeping one ear open for predators. And then her tongue stretched out as far as it could go and touched my hollow place. Dabbing and tasting, before lapping like a dog that's recognized its master. Long enthusiastic licks, each one ending up by slipping across my clit, sending shuddering signals through my semi-mortal frame and a squeaking sigh from my throat. I had little control over this, though I blushed to think anyone might overhear.

Again and again she licked me. Noisily, slurping between my tough thighs and I wriggled and it was fascinating. Relentless, might be one word I'd use for her. Another might be determined. Maybe she really believed that I was Artemis, or that if I were to be exhausted by the strength of her lust, by the cunning of her tongue, then maybe I'd put in a good word with the real Artemis. I don't know. All sorts of thoughts were sweeping through my brain right then. Not all of them made perfect sense.

Before I knew it she had a number of fingers lodged inside me. I hadn't seen her planning anything like it, and I couldn't count them right then, but suddenly I felt filled up. Stretched and fucked and she was sucking on my clit and I was in the air and scratching and squeezing at my own breasts. Absolutely fascinating.

The little bower echoed with wet noises as she slapped her hand in and out of my cunt and as she suckled on my clit as if it were a teat and she a piglet. I suddenly remembered the waterfall above Artemis's pool, that plunged down over the rocks. It wasn't a huge fall, but high enough to cause violence to the water that met it, to churn the far edge of the pool into a white froth. I felt like the water did as it approached the precipice above, as it slid along as it always had over the shingle and sand of the river bed, how it flew, free for a sudden, twirling and hurtling in the air, like the moment of freefall at the top

of a high swing, and then the plunge, the fall, the descent, the headlong, helpless collapse and the froth, the spume, the maelstrom at the bottom of it all and then again the calm as you swirled around Artemis's legs.

Callisto lay silent and I heaved, still feeling little electric aftershocks. She edged up the mossy bed to lie her head on my shoulder. Her arm snaked across my chest, embraced me, held me tight. I was hers, she thought.

I didn't think it my place that night to make love to her, to give her her orgasm. It was enough for her to be able to service her god, her lover, her Artemis. She didn't need anything more than that herself, that little nymph, that sweet Callisto. She had done good and as she slept I could tell that she loved me more than anything. Loved Artemis more than anything, would sacrifice herself for me, for her.

It was so sad. She reminded me of someone. It was so sad. I couldn't, right then, remember who.

When the morning came, obviously, I'd gone and Callisto found her way back to the camp where the merry band were camped. What happened then I don't know. Whether she looked across the fire at Artemis and smiled knowingly, and whether Artemis gave her a puzzled look back I can't say.

I don't know how Callisto dealt with the rejection that must've met her – silent or explicit. But nymphs are only mortal and such things as rejection pass in time. With death all things pass. I envy mortals that, sometimes.

So I'd been 'saved' from that bear, last night, by my dear daughter Artemis, and as we stood there, staring in a friendly if somewhat wordless manner at each other (she's never been a great conversationalist) I thought of that other night and just exactly what it was she was missing out on by never taking any of her nymphs up on their heartfelt offers. And I really felt quite sorry for the poor girl, the stupid girl.

Maybe I'll fuck another one of her nymphs one of these days. Get one of them to fuck me.

# Then: Four

Back then I took time to explore Semele, I stopped time. We lay in the long night and touched each other. We spoke, talked. She had dreams, thoughts. Bigger than a mortal should have, bolder and braver. She wasn't the sort to be gainsaid or ignored.

Her eyes sparkled as she spoke and her hands filled the room, the air, the space with shapes and swirls and movement. A whole theatre-world emerged above the bed, with players and plots that she'd been shaping inside herself for years. I think she loved me because I listened, because she'd found someone who didn't just nod assent and forget her as soon as they turned away. Everyone needs someone to take them seriously, I think, and I took her seriously. I loved her so much that I'd've granted her the world, the moon, any crown she wished had she but asked for it.

I listened and listened and sometimes I spoke, but that was harder. I didn't like that so much, because I couldn't tell her all the truth, I couldn't spill open the secrets of the universe to her. For a start she wouldn't have understood, not with that flesh and blood brain, and I wouldn't have been able to explain it all, not with the flesh and blood brain I had. But also it would've caused more harm than good, sharing secrets like that.

She knew what I was and that dazzled her enough. She was smart and however good my disguises were she'd see through them, see that something glowed underneath, that something about the body didn't quite fit the breath inside. But that's not why she loved me, not because of my divine nature, no. She loved me from when we'd first met, when she had no suspicions at all. She told me that. She would have loved me even if I'd been mortal, she said, even if I couldn't make the night last as long as it needed to last, even if I couldn't changed my body to suit her whims, even if I couldn't conjure fruit and meat from dust or wine from the air. She'd've loved me forever even if I'd just been a man, she said.

And, oh!, I loved her. Lying in that bed, under those blankets holding her to me, holding me to her. We were so happy. I loved to listen to her, in the dark, whispering her deepest thoughts, her secret thoughts, her sleepy, drowsy unconnected thoughts into my ear. Her cheek on mine, her mouth opening and closing and moving air across my new skin, my new flesh. I couldn't help but love her and she couldn't help but love me. The world had been made for this, it seemed. Even I, the King of Heaven, hadn't expected ever to be swept away like this when the world began. But the emotions of this human body, the chemicals of love that pulsed up and down the veins and arteries, that infiltrated the brain, the neurons, that leapt the synapses with their messages of hope – these emotions leaked out of the body and suffused my very nature, they coloured the core of me, so that when I was in The Palace, disembodied, eternal, I still couldn't help but think of Semele on Earth. I couldn't do anything but love her.

My arms would wrap around her, my stomach nestled in her back, our legs sliding around each other, my arms holding her breasts, her chest, my chin resting in her hair, on her neck. I'd hold her and listen to her talk in the night. Oh, I loved to hear her talk, but I loved her most when she shut up.

I was delighted by how similar the world looks on its many levels, how the body is so reminiscent of a landscape touched from a distance, seen from the air. How they each roll and undulate. Her stomach was like wheat-fields, like slow hillsides stroked by the sunlight on a long summer's afternoon. I spent hours gazing at it, laying out footpaths with my fingertips, astonished by how entrancing such a plain plane might be.

But it was a narrow land too, and either side of it there was a sloping fall, a curving cliff-tumble down her sides. And there my fingers teased and tickled and pulled forth hidden giggles and laughter and desperate escape routes as she begged me to stop in that voice that says, on a deeper level, don't stop. I could take her flank in one hand, thumb stroking her stomach, fingertips reaching under her to spread across her back and it was as if for a moment I were about to pick her up and lift her, haul her off somewhere else with one hand. It was as if I owned something for once.

Oh, I never recovered from love for her. The mystery of her travels before me still. I learnt to respect the physical with her, to worship the body, this tiny fleshy box and the marvellous things that it somehow managed to do. How it could feel. Oh, there is no passion without blood, without heart. And she had it all.

I'd worship between her thighs. I'd lie myself down before her and place my mouth in a kiss on that nether-mouth of hers, open those flowery dark lips with my tongue, drink of the pink depths of her. I could spend hours perhaps humbled in devotion, tipping her over peak after peak. She would clutch me, try to pull me away, but again it was the sort of Stop that was no sort of Stop at all. And she plunged and plunged, rolling with each flick, each kiss on her little rosebud hidden in that inverted v of skin. Oh, how I loved her and how she loved me.

And at other times we'd just lie together, handling each other's sex slowly, lazily as we kissed and nibbled. I'd stroke her breasts with their fat brown nipples swelling and sinking with the flow of blood, of contentment, of longing. I'd lean over and suck them as she gripped my cock in her small palm. We'd kiss some more, stare up at the stars wheeling overhead, the Milky Way flung across the sky like a spurt of spilt come. She'd wonder how long there was until dawn rose and I'd just fold time back another hour, put off the inevitable by another hour.

I'd ride my finger through the sluice of her wetness, swim back up above the dam, above the weir and ride down again. She was as slick as olive oil and as sweet as nectar. I'd run my finger time and again along the alley of her valley, from back to front, dragging its companions along the raised outer walls of that deep dyke, that ditch. Beautiful Semele would sigh with each stroke, as if the feelings sent up her spine, those leys joining cunt and clit and nipples and spine and brain, were unexpected every time. I'd dip my finger between her petals with each sliding, slit-loving stroke and splash through her juice.

It dribbled from her, droplets sticking in her hair, rivulets running their ways across her arse. Her thighs grew damp with the mist of her very self. My damp finger I'd raise to my lips and taste and return to the runnel of her cunny. Sometimes I'd paint her lips with her water, sometimes outline her nipples. I'd draw invisible patterns across her body, let the night wind dry her. Streams evaporating. A pool I filled in her navel slowly drying up like a sea grown too salty for its own good, except without the salt.

Hours later I'd kiss her, nuzzle on her breasts and discover the flavour her cunt, still rich, still bright and sweet, but unexpected in those places and potent. I'd twitch in her hand.

Sometimes she'd stroke me, sometimes she'd lick me, kiss me and sometimes we'd make love. And with each coupling our love grew stronger and longer and deeper and we swore vows to one another, spoke sentences that contained foolish words like forever and always and never.

One night I let her sleep until dawn came. She was tired. I was tired. I stood and watched her snoring gently, the blanket rising and falling. A single loose strand of hair crossing her cheek, fluttering in front of her mouth with each deep exhalation. Her ear was caught in a shaft of the last moonlight, looked as curled and folded and secretive as the mouth of her cunt. The dark hole at the centre leading, in each case, to hidden pleasures, to places that could be visualised, but never known as real topology: the brain and the womb.

She excited me so, just by being, just by breathing that I took my penis in hand (it was rarely less than semi-hard, and right now was firm and thick rather than ramrod stiff) and stroked it back and forth, riding the contours of an approaching orgasm, teasing it and slowing down, before surprising it, just as it was beginning to fade, with a burst of vigour. I could keep it on edge and panting for hours if I wanted, but dawn was nearly here and she wouldn't appreciate being stalled any longer. I looked at Semele's lips, at her closed eyes, imagining the strange orbs underneath (who ever invented such strangely sensitive and fragile organs of sense?), at her cunt-ish ear. Everything about her excited me as I masturbated that golden cock I'd built for her just the evening before.

She described what she wanted and I built it. Each night she tried a different shape, length, width. She tried shafts that tapered to a point, shafts that had fat bulbous heads that forced her open and then gave her a breath of relief as they popped through the archway of her mouth or cunt. She tried out different curvatures. She tried the poker straight. I delighted in her scientific mind. I imagined her making notes, keeping tallies and drawing graphs and charts, but I don't think she ever did. She asked for different bodies, faces too. There was nothing I wouldn't do for her.

As I came silently I caught my shimmering come in my hand and knelt beside her. As she snored quietly, savouring dreams even I couldn't touch, I dabbed her lips with my mighty seed. With one finger I slipped the taste of me inside her mouth, touched it to the tip of her tongue. Perhaps the scent of me infiltrated that dream, perhaps it didn't. I don't know. I never asked. But to know that we were so linked, that she wore me in her sleep like a ring on her finger, like the brooch on her cloak... ah, that meant something to me.

\*

That morning I vanished myself from the world with a heavy heart. Not because I believed it would be the last time I saw her, because it wasn't, but because she'd asked again that one question that I couldn't easily answer, and I knew soon she would become unbearable. I loved her and I feared that day. I feared what might happen.

'Show me what you really are,' she'd said.

'I can't,' I'd replied, 'It doesn't work like that.'

'But I love you, I want to know the real you,' she'd said.

'This is the real me,' I'd said, hitting my chest with my open palm.

'It's a body,' she'd said, 'You wear them like clothes. I love them all, but I want to see you naked, like you see me.'

'I can't do that,' I'd said, rather lamely, 'It wouldn't work. I'm too great.'

She'd been quite quiet, leant up on one arm, head resting in her hand. I'd looked at her heavy breasts as they lolled at a strange angle. The human body is very silly, as well as very beautiful, I'd thought to myself, and I had smiled inwardly.

'If you really loved me,' she'd said, 'You'd show me.'

I'd heard the gauntlet thrown down with those words and I feared it.

Then later we made love, we'd kissed and clung together, and then later still I'd left her in the path of dawn's chariot. Left her to go back to her life as I went back to mine, two lovers parted by the need to be getting on with other things. How prosaic.

# Now: Four

Now, someone pointed Perseus out to me last night. One of those demigod heroes going round doing heroic things and fulfilling all sorts of fateful prophecies on behalf of bored storytellers in The Palace. Apparently he was one of mine, so the stories went anyway, so I stepped down eighteen years earlier to do my own bit of fulfilling.

Humans are forever listening to prophecies and doing stupid things. Take this typical idiot-fellow Acrisius. Someone told him his daughter's son would kill him, so he locked her up with the intention that she could never have a son and thus, presumably, he'd never get killed. Well, had the chap never read a tragedy? Had he never seen a play? Why not just kill her at once and be safely done with it?

But no, for some reason he locked her underground in a specially constructed dungeon. Not a grotty dungeon, but still, not exactly luxurious. It was lined with copper. Underground and lined with copper to stop, well presumably things like me getting in to see her, I assume. But why a copper wall should provide any sort of barrier to a supernatural incorporeal omnipotent spirit-being I can't think.

But far be it for me to pick holes in her father's paranoid delusions. I acted as if the copper were a barrier, as if I couldn't just manifest in that room using the air to make me a body as easily as saying something simple. No, I played along with his preventative magics and instead went in through the door.

He had a guard constantly outside the door. Not the same

one all day, they swapped over, obviously. So all I did was sneak the key from Acrisius' belt as he slept, pop it into the hand of the chap outside Danaë's cell and then slip inside his head and take charge of his body.

I unlocked the door and slipped in.

The room was small. There was a comfy bed, with clean linen on it in one corner. A table and chair in the other. A commode beside the doorway. All the comforts of prison. On the table a lamp burnt, casting an ugly dim light across everything.

Danaë sat in the chair at the table reading. She turned round as I opened the door.

'It's you,' she said.

'Yes,' I replied.

'Have you got my dinner?'

'No.'

'Oh?' She looked curiously at me. 'What is it then? Has the old man finally seen sense?'

Her face brightened with a hopefully look, but then slumped back into a frown as I shook my head.

'No,' I said.

I shut the door behind me.

'What is it then?'

'Ah, well,' I began, stepping towards her and untying my tunic, 'There's a little matter of a prophecy to deal with.'

'What?' she said, standing up, 'What do you mean?'

She edged away, placing the chair between us. I think she was afraid.

'The future,' I said, growing bored of all this talk.

I shrugged the guard's tunic to the ground and put my hand on the back of the chair, pulling it aside.

'No, look,' she began, finding a bravura in her voice that

didn't match the uncertainty of her eyes, 'My father will kill you if you lay a hand on me... you know that...'

I stepped closer. The advantage of a small room like this was there was very little space for her to run in. The human body I'd borrowed, that I was steering, clearly had been thinking about something like this on all those long hours of guard duty outside because it had grown hard already. Me, I've never much enjoyed a duty-fuck, so I was grateful for my host's encouragement.

On the other hand, Danaë was giving no encouragement at all.

'I'll scream,' she threatened, 'I'll fight...'

I crossed the small space between us and took her hair in one borrowed hand and pulled her head to one side while with the other I reached down to take hold of this new cock I'd gained.

It was smaller than I'd've made it for myself, had I been choosing, but it would do. It was hot as a bonfire and hard as a little poker and the skin shifted happily under my palm.

I looked at her face as I twisted her to and fro.

She was pretty, with curling dark hair, but she'd grown pale and thin locked away underground. I don't understand humans sometimes, how they can do something like this to the ones they love. Acrisius would gain nothing in the long run, since everyone knows the Fates always get their way. He'd gain nothing but a sickly looking, underfed, weak daughter who hated him.

I felt so sorry for her, my heart almost burst with it. The poor thing.

If there weren't already another fate set up for her father, I might've devised something myself.

I looked at her eyes, which were angry, which were fearful and then pushed her to the ground. I had a job to do, stories to keep straight. I didn't have time or heart to make this last longer than necessary.

She crumpled to the floor in front of me. On her knees, half-resting on one hand. Her face level with this little guard cock that I was stroking. The guard's mind itched beside my own, watching out of his eyes, unable to move, unable to change anything.

She stared at me, at my belly, at the guard's belly. She leaned away from each thrust of the penis, each slap of my fist against my body. She was watching closely, not smiling but not crying. My hand still wrapped in her hair and held her close to me.

This little body, this frail human shell I was wearing was reaching its climax already, so soon and I felt embarrassed as it surprised me by shooting its load down the front of her smock. A little of the sticky come splashed her neck, but most of it stained the front of her dress. We both knew that that wouldn't come out.

As I'd jerked and spurted on her, she'd edged backward and let out a sound that was perhaps a sigh of relief. She seemed to be able to gain her composure better and quicker than I could and before the susurrations of orgasm had died out in the guard she spoke.

'Well, if you're all done,' she said with a haughtier tone than someone with such a grotty locking smock should by rights have had, 'then maybe you would leave.'

She had a point and I stepped out of the guard's body. It had been a plan and I'd liked the idea of it, but now it had backfired. He collapsed in a sleeping heap and I made a body for myself out of stray atoms I found lying around the place. A body much more suitable to one of my standing.

She gasped as the light of my transformation flooded the room, raised a hand to cover her eyes. But still she was proud.

'I don't care who you are,' she shouted into the dazzle, 'Get out. Now!'

Oh dear, I thought, far too proud for her own good.

I pulled her up to her feet and threw her onto the bed.

She lay on her back on the hard mattress and was trying to catch her breath as I stepped over her. Her smock had ridden up around her belly and the dark triangle of her cunt lay at the top of her locked thighs. With a little manipulation of the universe I spread her legs open. She struggled against it, but my control of the fundamental forces overrode any pressures her muscles could make in reply.

With one hand she covered herself and with the other she tried to pull down her clothes, either way to protect her modesty. But with a mighty golden hand I swept her efforts aside. I couldn't be doing with this coyness, not now. I pinned her hands above her head as she writhed and tried to break free.

Her eyes were locked with mine. If she was going to be fucked, she seemed be saying, at least she'd see who was doing it and remind them that she was there, that she wasn't a part of it, that she was still free inside herself.

Well, that was fine by me, I thought, as I picked up my heavenly penis in my right hand and juggled it a little.

Compared to the human cock of the guard, the pretty little thing he'd kept hidden away under his tunic, this one I'd made myself was mighty, heavy and weighty. It felt gorgeous and I longed to have it in my own mouth, to feel the full power of it. I envied those who got to play with it.

Stepping forward I pressed it against the wide-spread cunt of this haughty vessel of the Fates. Danaë screamed and wriggled, but so far underground, with her guard sleeping the sleep of the just in the corner, she was perfectly free from rescue. Her father had clearly thought things through before he'd locked her away down her. A truly wise man, you might say. Or an absolute ignorant fool. Sometimes it's a very thin line between the two.

I rubbed the moist tip of my phallus against the little pink lips that hid between the fur and she bucked, fearful of what would happen next. She'd seen the size of me, perhaps.

She shouted the most obscene curses, implored my brothers and sisters to stop this. At one point she even called on me, not knowing it was I who was already there. But she made such a fuss, moved so violently that I grew tired with these games and stood up over the bed, between her legs, but a step back from her.

'Well, look,' I said to her, 'If you're not going to enjoy yourself, then just lie still and shut up. I'm only doing my job here, you know? We've all got roles to play. What do you think, that you're something special?'

She looked at me as I said this, locked eyes again and with a scorn that I could feel spat an answer back at me.

'Fuck you, Your Highness,' she said.

Oh well, that was it. I couldn't be doing with such cheek. I hadn't much wanted to come down here tonight in the first place, I thought to myself, let's just get out of here.

But before I did I aimed that golden member of mine right at her pouting, unhappy little cunt and let gush a jet of piss that played across her lips and her thighs, splashing up over the bed. I focussed on her clitoris, sending involuntary shivers

of pleasure through her nervous system, making her gasp. I sprayed my godly pee up her belly, hammering on the roof of her womb, I played it under her buttocks, tickling her arse and I pointed it into her cunt. I played with her lovely little lips there, flicking them this way and that, tickling them as if my stream of golden water was a tongue, then I penetrated her with piss like a penis, a swift fertile stream, relentless in its pressure, gushing right up her cunt, filling her up so full that she leaked and pissed herself for whole minutes after I'd vanished myself out of there.

As I wisped myself to nothing, letting the room fall back to the dimness it had been in before, I watched her breathing heavily on the bed, lying in pee, resting her hand on her sodden pussy as if I'd just exhausted her. She pulled her smock down to cover herself as I whisked the guard back outside, leaving Acrisius' key in his hand, a foggy memory in his head and empty flask of wine at his side.

Let those wretched ungrateful unfriendly mortals work out a story to tell the ages after that one.

# Then: Five

I'd never really known fear before. I'd been angry, I'd done that once or twice, and I'd been distracted, and I was in love. But fear had never really been a part of what I was about.

What does a god have to fear? I **am** the natural forces. I **am** the unexpected occurrences and calamities. I know the provenance of all accidents and their explanations. The future and past is open to me like a painting, if I care to look at it.

I knew what was going to happen. I knew it. And I couldn't change it. Perhaps I could delay it, but there was no change available, no last minute chances or divine intervention on my part.

And all the same, I was scared. Inevitability did nothing to curb the panic that was muttering in this mortal gut, that felt like a breathless lump of ore in my heart, filling my lungs so no inhalation ever satisfied.

Tonight was the night. By morning, I knew, my love would be lost. She'd be gone. I'd seen my own future stretching out before me, eternity after eternity, without her and it would begin with the next dawn.

She had no inkling.

She lay on top of me that evening, kissed me, rested herself on my belly as if she hadn't a care in the world. Her breasts hung above my chest. As she moved I could feel them brush against me, feel their weight settle for a moment in one place, lift and move off again. Her eyes closed and her hands gripped my arms which sprawled somewhere above my head.

We lay like that for a long time. I was full and filling inside her. My spreading penis was sat snug in her cunt, savouring its last night of safety and security. It was warm in there, dark and snug and it smelt of home. Hell, it was home. Whenever I'd been linked to this woman, in just this way, it had always been as if something had gone right in the world. For once I was a part of something bigger, and I was in the right place. It's hard to explain, but settled in a mortal body, and with that mortal body stuck inside another, it was as if I were real for once.

Oh, it's all very well being in charge. All very well being able to do most anything. But Semele loved me for being less than I was. She would put her arms around me, open her legs to me and let me be human. This was never possible with Hera. There is no equivalent to this intimacy in The Palace; no equivalent to this nudity. Only in these tiny mortal bodies, on this thin physical plane can there be secrets. Only here can the inhabitants not know one another in the slightest. For Semele to know something about me I had to tell her. For me to know about her she had to tell me. This is what words were made for, why writing will catch on. For human beings to know one another they must speak and write and actually make the effort. And so they keep secrets, they distrust each other, they lie and dissemble and hide things. They betray one another and steal and cheat and they tell the truth. They write poems and paeans and make a statement of their loves, their fears, their angers. They must always act in order to be known, and sometimes the laying down of words can be act enough.

Whenever I was with Semele she would talk to me. I listened and with each sentence she uttered I loved her more. She revealed herself to me, more so than by ever opening her thighs, with her words. Anyone could have taken her, could have fucked her, by force or otherwise, but no compulsion could ever have persuaded her to open her mind, her heart up to them. Only to me and only because she loved me.

That last night I held her close and listened as she whispered.

Each word was a gift and a step closer to the end. Each word refilled my heart and emptied it out again, was a torment and a treasure.

At some point in the early hours I rolled her over, still with my shaft deep inside her, as it had been for hours, slowly pulsing, slowly twisting and shifting, keeping her alive and awake to it, keeping her on edge. At some point I rolled her over and in a frenzy pounded into her. It was in anticipation of the end. A maddening helpless feeling was welling up in me and I had to try to exorcise it somehow and I took it out on her. Thumping like a madman, like a crazy, I thrust in and in and in. She cried out with the force of it. Her legs fell open and her fingers dug deep trenches in my shoulders. Her breath pumped out of her with yelps and tears and I pinned her arms down and mindlessly fucked away.

In just minutes I came. Filling her belly with my boiling, swirling seed.

I collapsed on top of her. Exhausted, but not satisfied. Our sweat mingled in the air and as I rolled off she whimpered and moved limply trying to get comfortable.

Angry with myself for giving in to such violence and passion, angry for having looked to her as a channel for my own confused feelings, I reached out to stroke her. I wanted to take her in my arms, show her the gentler side again, remind her of the man she loved. And I did. I held her, stroking, calming, soothing her with kind words and warm fingers until the stars dimmed on the horizon and the birds had long since begun their welcome to the new day.

*

'I worry,' she says.

'I know,' I say.

'I don't know you,' she says.

'I know,' I say.

'I love you,' she says, 'But I don't really know you, do I?'

'No,' I say, 'But you know what's important.'

'I worry,' she says again, 'I want to know you,'

'I know,' I say.

And the conversation goes round again. We've had this talk, this discussion so many times I forget when it first happened. The request is always the same. And my answer is always the same too.

It's the difference between me and her, between her and me. The one hurdle that will always keep us apart. She talks to me, tells me about herself, lets me see, in words and actions, inside her. By watching her, by listening to her, by trusting her I have come to understand her. I can predict what she'll say next, in a wide variety of situations. I love the way she follows simple patterns and then forgets them, does something unexpected. But even the unexpected is her. She's beautiful and wonderful in her being human, in her being what she is. Her nature is something glorious, because it is uniquely her and it is so small, packed inside this single fleshy walking box. The moment it vanishes she vanishes too, from the world, from forever. She is so special because of that.

Me, on the other hand... well, I will never vanish entirely. I'm not limited in that way. Not confined, except on earth, in mortal shape. But then my will still flies free, outside. It is bigger than the world always. She can never know that. She can only ever comprehend the smallest corner of my majesty, of my soul, if you will. She can only be allowed to know me in whichever mortal shape she asks for tonight.

But she wants more. She wants to know.

And this is the request that comes night after night. And I know, because I love her so, that I can't keep refusing her. Can't keep my real nature hidden away forever.

I have told her to be satisfied with what I give, but she's not. And I understand that.

So this morning, as the birds sing and the sun rises, I give in to her wish. For her and her alone I shrug off this mortal mantel I'm wearing like a cloak and stand before her awful and naked and unrestrained.

The clouds flood in, the earth trembles and shakes and the grass withers. Leaves are swept off the trees in a whirlwind and lightning crashes down obliterating her from the world. In an instant she is reduced to dust, to ashes in the atmosphere. Miles up she freezes, dispersed over countries, and eventually falls across distant lands.

In an instant I tuck myself away, pull up a hasty semi-mortal form, reduce myself and lock myself in. Limit myself once again and from the whirlwind I snatch a germ, a seed that was flung from her womb – our son, who will grow in The Palace, but make his home in the world.

# Postscript

I can't forgive myself for this thing. And I can't forget that she insisted on it.

Several thousands of years after she was obliterated a poet in a northern land wrote, under a grey sky of rain and cloud, lines that seem apt to me. 'Yet each man kills the thing he loves, / By each let this be heard, / Some do it with a bitter look, / Some with a flattering word. / The coward does it with a kiss, / The brave man with a sword!'

As ever, the poets have it right.

I hated Semele, long after I loved her. We had a time together, but we had an eternity apart, and it was all her fault. I blamed her more than anything. I blamed her more than anyone. If only she'd been less curious. If only she hadn't wanted to know everything. If only she hadn't loved me so. (If only she'd been less human.)

I could have left her. One morning I could have gone and never returned. That's true. She'd've lived. That's true.

But she would've died inside. Love does that to a women. That and abandonment. How could I have walked away? From my place beside Hera's throne I'd've looked down and seen her. Seen her weeping, worrying and wondering where I was. She would blame herself, as I blame her now. What did I do, she'd say, to drive him away? And I could never give her an answer, for to go and see her, to speak to her, even through the diffuseness of oracles and omens, would be to fall under her spell again. Because that's what love is, I've decided: a sort of spell.

I had no choice but to do as she asked. In the end.
I'd've done anything for her.
In fact I did.

*

And now? Well, now I search for her, don't I? Every step on Earth is filled with longing for her, memories of her. No one knows me the way she did. No one ever will.

This pain she left me with, that surges even in the spirit, keeps us together.

*

It's stupid, I know. It's all stupid. All this fuss over a mortal, over a woman? Sometimes I exaggerate things, for dramatic purposes. Sometimes I get carried away with my own rhetoric. Ignore me when that happens.

Women are, after all, just women and mortals are, after all, just mortals and the supply is almost endless, almost limitless. I have eternity and energy and unlimited willpower. I am free of responsibilities and the world is my playground.

Here I come.

*A Cretan Story*

# Minotaur

It is easy to forget that like bears,
like men and like women,
like children and cats and dogs
and like mice in their burrows
even this Minotaur must sleep.

Heaving breaths over its shoulder,
like a man at work on the road
shovelling steaming bitumen,
it grunts its way through the night
curled like a baby under a sheet.

Somewhere it has a mother
and perhaps tonight she sneaks out,
down from the palace
and with thread and love
navigates to the heart of this labyrinth.

Pausing in the doorway
a shaft of moonlight falls
from a high window across her face,
along the floor, to the bed.
She watches.

It's not so bad. There's a bed, not straw.
There are sheets, not rags.
She's had her way in small ways,
saved up what pride she could afford,
protected the dignities she could.

Lacking the right lips or cords or brain
he has never spoken,
but she imagines somewhere in the dark
there is a glimmer of thanks,
an understanding of the word 'mother'.

He tosses over. A sleeping bellow.
Sheets brush aside
and his hairy wide body is exposed,
his hands, the meat between his legs,
thick and animal.

# One: Pasiphaë Speaks

### i.

He was my boy. That's how I thought of him. And I was the only one who cared enough, who took the time to care for him. I understood, of course, why he was whispered about and why he was shut away. I agreed, too. But what fault there was, what crime had been committed, well, it wasn't his. He was just a boy, just an innocent little boy.

Some nights I'd creep out of the palace in the early hours and thread my way into his maze, pass through doors that no one but the architect and I knew of, until I found myself in the alcove outside his small room. Hiding the light of my lamp with my hand, the noise of his heavy, brutish breathing would fill the darkness and sometimes I would just stand and listen, knowing he was asleep, not wishing to disturb him. But at other times I'd tiptoe into his chamber, set the lamp down by the door and climb onto his pallet with him. I'd slip my thin neck under his massive arm, press my ear to his massive chest and recognise my boy's heartbeat, as distinct and honest as a fingerprint and I'd know that everything was all right for an hour or two.

Later I'd slip away, before dawn, and make my way back to the palace by secret paths. Back to my own chamber where sometimes my maid would be waiting anxiously, but I'd silence her with a gesture and she'd brush out my hair and the sun would rise and another day of duty and etiquette would unfold. But even as I sat sewing or listened in on one of my husband's trade discussions I would remember that rough, hot breath of my boy on my neck and I'd blush, quiver and smile to myself.

## ii.

It had all started years before when my husband had made a pact with the gods to become king of this island. Everything had worked out and I stood by his side, so proud, on that day when the crown was first rested on his temples and the sun shone on us both amid the cheers and trumpeting of the crowds. We went inside and there was a feast such as I'd never seen before and merchants from over the seas had brought strange foods and gifts which they laid before us. I shared in his triumph, in his achievement, sitting quietly by his side, smiling quietly.

But of course he had a fault. And as is not uncommon it was greed. The gift he'd been sent by Poseidon as a token of his support, and which my husband had been meant to give back once the job had been done, well, he'd decided to keep it. If I'd been stronger tongued back then, if I'd only had the mind to speak my will, to stand up to my man and tell him the future, I would have done so in an instant. As it was I didn't know the future. I thought he knew best. I knew no better. And the punishment that should have been his, by the capriciousness of the bastard gods, fell on my shoulders. Oh, the shame was his too, but the acts were entirely mine.

Poseidon had provided my husband with a bullock of such immensity that no one had seen the like. No wonder he decided to keep it. People came from miles to point and stare at this mad monster of a bull down on the beach. It snorted and pawed at the sand and glowered at anyone who came near. It would make runs toward the crowd that gathered, turning aside at the last moment as they scattered and fled. Proving to itself just who was the master here, but being puzzled all the same. It didn't know how it had come to be here or where here was. It was a dumb animal, conjured out of nothing by a thoughtless god, but filled with an awareness and a life and dumped down on this beach. Like all of us, I guess, it was just trying to understand itself and to prove that it was master of its own fate.

My heart weakened every time I saw the poor thing. I wept whenever some traveller pointed and jeered at it or threw stones. The crowds lacked compassion. To them a monstrous bull was just a freak and an entertainment, but to me it was a marvel. I would shout at the visitors, at the tourists. I'd ask them not to be so cruel, to leave the poor thing alone. He was far from home and confused and needed care, not abuse. Of course they listened to me, I was the queen after all, but as soon as my back was turned I'd hear the roar of the crowd, the roar of my bull and I knew I was once again powerless.

My husband didn't understand the interest I took in his prize, but he acceded to my request to punish those members of the public who toyed with it. He wanted to protect his beast while he decided what to do with it, just as I wanted to protect it for my own sentimental reasons. There were a few executions, whippings and fines, and in time the crowds grew weary of this giant bull that did nothing but bellow and pace about, always looking out to sea as if it might find its answers there.

I stood alone on the beach then, just me and the beast. From the distance I would sigh as I caught the glint of the sun on its huge brown eyes, as I watched the glorious muscles shift beneath the skin. When I thought of the power there was in there, when I thought of the sheer brutality of this lovely thing

I shuddered and grew excited. Whatever my husband was he was just a man.

But when I stepped close to lay a hand on the flank, to actually feel the energy, it would roar and lower its horns at me, take a dangerous step. I'd skip backwards, off of its patch of beach. It was a wild animal, violent and terrifying in its otherness. Whatever set my heart beating, and started the honey between my thighs flowing, was not human. It was massive and astonishing and I realised with relief that I had fallen in love.

## iii.

My dreams were filled with snorting and weight and heat and I'd wake up sweating and quite undone by the thought of that tragic beast all alone on the shore. It was so sad to know it was alone in the world, unable to voice its wishes or desires, unable to escape to somewhere, anywhere, of its own choosing, and unable, in its bull brain to know that it was loved. What could I do for this beast except devote my life to caring for it? I could have a golden shelter built for it out of the wind and the sun. I could order the finest foods for it. I could see that it was tended by the wisest of our apothecaries if it grew ill. Oh, I could do all this, but this love I felt wasn't just a longing for the monster's well-being, it was an animal itch all of its own.

I approached my husband's handyman, the inventor Daedalus, with the problem. He adored a challenge and immediately set to work thinking about the matter. The main problem was that the monstrous bull felt such antipathy toward humans, it seemed, that approaching it at all was dangerous. It was impossible to drug its feed, because it seemed to subsist on nothing but the air and sea, and wouldn't touch the ordinary fodder which had been left for it.

Night after night he showed me pieces of paper covered with plans and theories and we settled on the most straightforward of the lot: disguise. While he set about building his articulated wooden cow frame, I had long conversations with my sister Circe about magic and enchantments. She knew more than I ever had about such things and has learned even more since those days. She concocted a love draught that would woo anything, she claimed. The scent of it would wisp up the bull's nostrils and click the switches in even its animal brain. I simply needed to get close enough.

# iv.

One evening Daedalus led me down to his workshop and showed me what he had built. It was a contraption. A life-size wooden cow thing that he imagined I could climb inside and wear like a suit. In it I would be able to walk around on all fours, my face pressed up inside the cow's head, gazing out of its mouth, my rear raised in the air pointing out of the aperture that he left open in the cow's rump. I'd been quite frank with him about the uses to which I intended to put his device and he'd gleefully worked with those necessities in mind.

I won't pretend that I was pleased when I saw it. It looked like a cow, but not in any way that would convince even a half blind idiot. It was wooden and metal; the joints were greased and polished, and nuts and bolts and screws glinted. It was all sharp angles and straight lines and failed to live up to the organic, breathing pictures I'd been filling my daydreams with. Even later on, when we'd covered it up with cow hides, the shape of the mechanics still showed through. It turned out, however, that bulls have little sense of the aesthetic.

Nevertheless I thanked Daedalus and I slipped off my dress to try his suit on. He'd arranged a set of steps on one side and lifted the hatchway in the thing's back and held my hand as I climbed inside. It was awkward and uncomfortable to wear. It was more than snug, but I managed to slide one leg into each of the rear legs and hook my ankles into the loops that kept them secure. The mound of my cunt rested on a padded surface and I knew the honey was flowing even as I thought about what the dreadful contraption might soon be bringing me.

I leant forwards, slipping one arm after the other down the tight passages that ran inside the forelimbs and resting my throat on the padded neck. My stomach and breasts lay flat on the polished wood of the inside and when Daedalus shut the roof on me I was squashed into place by further padding pushing down from above. I gripped the handles in the forelegs and tried to move.

The suit wouldn't move. It was too heavy and I was too weak. I could see through my limited field of vision the far side of his workshop and I could extend this view a little to either side by swinging my head. At least that worked. But I couldn't see Daedalus and if he were speaking to me I couldn't hear him. I tried to call out to him, but my face was squashed so snugly up in the cow-suit's throat that I could barely open my mouth wide enough to breathe, let alone shout out. I began to feel claustrophobic.

It was hot in the suit and the pressure on my body from every side was such that after a while I hardly noticed it. Instead the only part of me that was free, that was open to the cool evening air was my raised backside, pointing out of the open circle of the cow's rear. Wherever Daedalus was, whatever he was doing I knew that he had as perfectly framed a view of my pouting cunt and arsehole as my husband had ever had. There they were, raised up five feet off the floor, basking in the open air, unable to move. It was quite delicious, aside from the thought that soon I might get to couple with the monstrous thing that I loved (even then I knew that this love was quite inexplicable (or explicable only in the shape of some unnatural curse from the gods) but there was something inevitable about it all that I couldn't change), it was rather exciting all by itself to have the cool of the evening focussed on that one spot – while feeling was smothered throughout the rest of my body. I could feel the slightest draught lick across my lips and buttocks and I knew the way my legs were splayed inside the cow-frame must be parting my little upright mouth provocatively.

It was just as I was thinking thoughts like this and wondering when Daedalus would think to open me back up again, that I heard the door to his workshop open. Clearly I actually could hear through the hollows of the suit's neck and the inventor had just been keeping quiet as usual.

'Your highness,' he said.

My husband answered him.

It was quite astonishing to hide in plain sight like this. I hadn't told my king of my redirected desires, he wasn't the sort to have plunged into the project with the verve that the inventor had. Instead I can imagine the king being ashamed and locking me away somewhere until the phase had passed.

But there I was stark naked in the middle of Daedalus' workshop while my husband and he spoke only a few yards away. I knew that the door led the visitor to a side view of the cow-suit and was relieved to think that I neither had to look at the king, nor that he were facing my rump, eye to eye as it were. They spoke about this and that, plans for some party I seem to recall, and I could hear Daedalus kindly, but ineffectually, trying his hardest to subtly hurry his king up and get him away. After a while the conversation turned to the centrepiece of the workshop.

It wasn't strange or unusual for the most bizarre and farfetched things to be on display there (Daedalus worked constantly on projects that never came to fruition or which only he could understand), so a giant wooden cow was nothing extraordinary.

Daedalus explained in his usual half absent-minded way the rough reasons for creating such a suit – its (theoretical) ambulatory capabilities, the sly disguise to get close to querulous beasts. He didn't mention me, nor the mighty bullock on the beach. I heard the king laughing indulgently, as he often did (as we all often did) when Daedalus explained something that made perfect sense to him, but which to the rest of the world might be a little harder to grasp.

I heard him chuckle and then stop. He'd walked around the back of the suit and seen what there was to see.

'Oh, Daedalus,' he said, 'You didn't say you had someone in here already?'

'Er, yes, your highness, we were just testing it when you came in. It seems I've built the thing a little too heavy for the lady to lift.'

'So she's stuck in there?'

'For the moment, yes.'

The king laughed coarsely at this.

I blushed as my husband made some lewd, though complimentary, remarks about the wetness of my cunt and the pout of my arsehole, to which Daedalus mumbled some assent.

The thought of these two men gazing at my sex like that, off-hand and so matter-of-factly, the one knowing that he was looking at the other man's wife, made me ripple with a delicious, scared thrill. I'm sure a further trickle of honey coated my already slick slit.

'Anyone I know?' the king asked.

'Er, well...' Daedalus stuttered.

I couldn't think what my husband would say or do if he found me there in Daedalus' workshop stripped naked in a

wooden cow with my cunt on display to the handyman, and so I was relieved when the king drew his own conclusions.

'One of the maids is it? You've used... oh who was it? ...Mestra, I think, in some of your experiments?'

'Yes, your highness, that's true,' Daedalus said, carefully answering the second question and leaving the first to dangle.

'Well, just as long as they're fit for work in the morning... What's in my palace is yours, you know that.'

My husband held the inventor in high regard and had always been surprisingly indulgent with him. I don't doubt Daedalus has helped the king in several amatory schemes over the years too.

'Oh yes, your highness, you're too kind.'

'Yes. Maybe,' the king answered.

And then, without a warning I felt hands touching me, pulling apart the lips of my cunt and sliding their way inside. I let out a puff of surprise and they quickly withdrew.

'Fetch me a stool,' the king said.

Then I felt, with less surprise, the head of his hard little cock pop inside me, as it had any number of times before. I wriggled my arse, but there was so little leeway available it had very little effect. Was I trying to evade him, or trying to encourage him? He was my husband after all, and my king, but, then again, he did imagine he was a fucking a parlour maid.

It was quite sweet, that little fuck, but it didn't last long. He was a king with weighty affairs of state on his hands, he always said, and had little time to spend on pleasure. I recognised the pattern of those quick thrusts in and out, and knew just the moment when he'd come. Each shallow thrust into me nudged open the mouth of my cunt and left the depths of it longing for something deeper, something harder, something further, but the depth of his entry was limited by the wooden frame through which his cock was thrust, and when he shot his load it spurted across my rear, spitting up on my arsehole and dribbling down along my pouting little lips. I could picture what it looked like and wondered what Daedalus was thinking of all this. Although he'd fled here to Crete with his son, he was a shy buffoonish sort of genius who I had never really imagined taking an interest in such things as spunk covered cunts, but, in the end, really, one never knows what people are thinking about.

I heard the king climb down and walk out of the workshop without saying a word. The door clicked shut behind him.

I honestly wondered if Daedalus might take advantage of the situation as my husband had done. I was still trapped in the frame, unable to move, freshly fucked and my lips were peeled open waiting for more. I imagined for a moment that he were the sort of man who would line all his friends up, one after the other and charge them a coin a head for a fuck of the cow-lady. There she is, strapped in, faceless and unable to escape you. Just a spitting, pouring hole or two ready to be filled – choose either my good friend. And maybe if I hadn't been his queen he might've done so. I wondered if I would've minded so much. Obviously I'd've had to have had him executed afterwards, but thinking of the free licence of such silly fucking had its own thrill to me.

As I weighed the morality of such an act I reflected that I was the woman in a wooden cow-suit she'd commissioned to be built in order to make love to the giant bullock she desired, so I might not be the best judge of the rights and wrongs of any given situation.

As all this flowed through my head I felt a cloth rubbing across my rear, cleaning the juice and sperm away with a gentle stroke and pat. I could almost see the inventor blushing as he did so. Then there was a pause and a click as the trapdoor opened above me and suddenly I felt the cold air on my back, and as I drew deep breaths, several of them in a row, I realised how constricted I had actually been in there.

With a gloved hand he reached under my shoulder and helped raise the front half of me out of its prison.

'I'm so sorry,' he said when my face was free.

I looked at him as I pulled myself out and climbed down the steps. My legs were wobbly as he held up my dress for me to climb into.

'I'm very sorry,' he repeated.

'He's my husband,' I said, 'I've always known he was a bastard philanderer, but that's just what it means to be king, isn't it?'

Daedalus looked puzzled for a moment, before he smiled.

'Oh, that. Yes, your highness. The king is what he is. That's true. But I meant, I'm sorry you couldn't lift the suit. It hasn't worked.' His face fell. 'I can try to find a lighter wood, perhaps, or maybe...'

I stopped him with a hand held to his mouth.

'Don't worry Daedalus,' I said, 'What can't be done with technology I'll do with witchcraft.'

'Yes your highness.'

He bowed and I left him and his cow-suit in order to go talk to Circe again.

## V.

Even back then Circe was constantly working on a variety of enchantments. She always had her nose in a book or her mortar in her pestle pestling away at a bunch of herbs. When I explained the problem she gave me a potion she just happened to have lying around in her laboratory that would increase my strength ten fold. I'd long ago learnt not to ask questions such as why she had such things to hand. Like Daedalus and his workshop, Circe's rooms were always filled with projects in progress, usually for no other reason than to change the world around. So far the world still exists so she can't have done too much damage, though I doubt everyone she's involved in her schemes might feel quite so generous.

As I was leaving her, she slipped another phial in my hand.

'You might appreciate this,' she said, 'It's a sort of metamorphic relaxant. I think it might help.'

With that she shut her door in my face and went back to her inscrutable meddling.

## vi.

A few nights later I met with Daedalus on the shore. He had had the cow-suit hauled out of the workshop and set up a few hundred yards from the gruffly stomping bull. Even in the dark he couldn't stop his pacing to and fro. The poor love was impatient for the future to arrive, just as I was impatient for my future. At that moment I felt my heart beat in my chest fit to escape, and I knew that if only he would accept me we could live happily side by side. Nothing would stand in the way of our love. Not what people said, nor the way they stared, because we'd be there together in the face of it all. The only true sign that a love is a lasting love is the actual act of making it last, of seeing the years through hand in hand, of being as close after thirty years as after three, of still feeling the same thrills pulse through you at the end of time as when you first met.

I was sure we would see off the naysayers with the simple fact of our continuing love.

Daedalus and his son stood by the cow-suit. He'd sent away the servants who'd carried the contraption out of his workshop before I arrived. He was always thoughtful like that. I handed his son my dress and Daedalus gave me his hand as I climbed up the steps and into the suit.

When my legs were settled inside the cow's legs and I was preparing to lie down I had him pass me the phials one at a time. I unplugged each one and gulped down the thick liquids that Circe had filled them with. I could feel the slow blunt trickle of them as they slid down my throat, seemingly oblivious to my efforts to swallow: they took their own time and seemed to move backwards and forwards inside me of their own volition. The effect was most unnerving, unpleasant but I trusted my sister implicitly. Well, sometimes.

As they penetrated further into the depths of me I bent forwards, sliding my arms down and leaning my throat in that of the cow. When Daedalus shut the lid on me I once again felt the cold night air focussed on my buttocks and more precisely on the splayed open apertures that peered out of the cow's arse into the dark.

I lifted one arm, testingly, and found that the cow shifted around me. Wooden muscles flexed, the limb rose and I felt a part of this thing. It was strange because it wasn't my shape. I'm not a natural quadruped, but with practice I learnt the order of the limbs, the right way to lift and walk and balance. I could feel the grit of the sand under my wooden hooves, I could feel the swell and contraction of my wooden muscles – muscles I myself didn't have. I could see and hear and smell, not through the narrow passage I knew my face pointed through, but through the senses of the suit itself, through the eyes it would have had had it been a real cow, and the same wooden ears. Circe's potions had done the job, it would seem. Not only was I able to steer and move the cow-suit, but it had leaked into me and I into it, so that we were linked together as a single creature.

I turned to look at Daedalus and his boy and they took a hurried little step backwards, as if they were afraid of me: astonished, yes, naturally, but afraid too. I paid them no more heed and instead began the long walk to that stretch of beach on which my love lived.

Here I came, a transformed woman. I had changed myself

for my man. I'd altered everything that seemed normal to me to fit in with his criteria of beauty. I'd left my world behind and joined his. I was his, that much I was certain of. His to order, to command, to take. And up to this point in time he hadn't even noticed me, not given me even a second glance, no more regard than he showed to the lowliest of the tourists who had stared and walked away from him. He had never seen me, but now that I had made the effort, now that I had made this commitment to him, he had to notice me at last. Surely, I thought, this must prove my unending love?

I strode with a purpose up the beach, creaking and groaning as the wooden muscles and tendons of my body shifted around me with each step. It was a comforting sound, a beautiful sound: the sound of me. My four legs felt strangely familiar as I stepped, the flex of the sap, the click and twist of the bolts, planks and hinges: I was at one time a mechanical thing and a living thing. A loving thing. I was a constructed thing given life. But while my limbs and my flanks and my senses were consumed in the fibre of the suit, in the very grain of the wood, my cunt, the one part of me open to the air, that was free of mechanical interference, throbbed with all the organic life I owned. Everything truly living seemed to be finding its relevance in the sweaty, honey covered slit. It pulsed in anticipation of love. It leaked with my desire. It pouted brazenly into the night, staring back, ever widening, at the inventor and his son as I strode away from them.

# vii.

When I came within twenty yards of my love, my goal, my man, he raised his head up and gave me more than a glance. Whenever I'd watched him before he'd stared dismissively or with distaste at the people who stared at him, but now there was something markedly different in his eye. He could tell, I could tell, that I wasn't just another gawping spectator, that I was someone who cared, someone who approached out of a selfless desire.

He never saw the person of me, only the cow of me. I felt his eyes rove over my shape, my great haunches as they swayed with each footstep. His eyes roamed over my shoulders which were strong and broad. I was no normal cow, he was realising, no simple scrawny beast of the Cretan landscape, parched with the sun and thinned by the scrubby food in the hills. I was mighty. I was the female equivalent of his mightiness. I could feel, even from the distance, something happening inside his little bullish brain. Something like love, perhaps. Circe's philtre's glamour was weaving its spell.

I stopped a short way from him and lowered my head. A suppliant act that I hoped would display to him my respect and my desire.

He bellowed.

I lowed.

As far as lover's declarations went we were breaching no new heights of poetry. But all the same it seemed that what was needed to be said was said. In his animal grunts, in his snorts, in the clouds of sand he raised up with his impatient stomping of the ground he displayed his urgent need for me. In my swaying, in my tentative steps forward, head lowered, nose reaching out to brush his, I answered his passion with passivity.

He had existed for so long on this beach, for months and months, without knowing a woman, without, perhaps, even knowing that such things as women existed. But when I appeared to him, when I swayed the bulk of my body up against his, everything changed for him. His masculinity was unlocked and his potential was fulfilled.

In a movement so sudden as it was surprising he raised himself up. He found his way behind me and heaved his otherworldly bulk up onto my back, wrapped a foreleg round each supple wooden flank and without a pause for thought, romance or an introduction, buried his vast shaft of bull-cock inside me.

Good gods! It made me cry out, in a human scream through the wooden mouth-aperture and in a bovine bellow through the magical glamour that entwined the suit and me. Never before or since have I been so full. Without finesse, without gentleness I was stuffed by that prick. (Through 'prick' is far too small a word to describe what he had, what I shared. In fact I can't think of any noun usually used to describe the male member that has the hugeness, the sheer physical weight behind it that that bull's piston did. After him everything else seemed ineffectual, superficial even: the world, indeed, had become a slighter place.) As he serviced me with his quick pumps I felt my entire body stretched beyond pleasure. I became for those moments simply cunt, every nerve ending, every firing, flaming distended bit of flesh, skin, muscle and mucous was alive with cunt.

I would have split, would have become the victim of an outrageous, embarrassing, disreputable death had Circe not dosed me up with her potions, had she not used her magics to make me pliable and infinitely accommodating. Nevertheless the pain of that intrusion was intense, I bucked my cow body back and forth, trying to escape from under my love's weight, to get away from his pinning grip, but I couldn't kick him off. He held me with his legs, kept himself on-board and buried his red-hot tool deeper into my womb. His teeth bit into the wood of my neck and I felt the chunk of carpentry he tore out as a sharp, painful relief from the intense chronic pain between my haunches.

In a way I felt a wistful longing for the shallow, human penetration of my husband, the king. His little cock held such appeal in that moment. The little thrusts that he had dealt me a few nights earlier when he found me trapped in the suit were not devoid of appreciation: I'd enjoyed the simplicity of them; and he'd enjoyed the coming and the thought that he was getting away with something. An illicit fuck always made him happy, I could tell. It lifted the weight of affairs from his shoulders for a half hour. But this bull with its giant cock was thoughtless, was empty of cognition – empty even of the understanding or appreciation of pleasure. It didn't care about what it was doing, it was just fulfilling the call of its nature.

Suddenly this was clear. The veil that the gods had fogged me for months with was lifted in a second and I was just a stupid, silly woman strapped inside a giant articulated wooden cow-suit being fucked to bruised little pieces by some monster raised up out of the sea.

There was no love here. There was just the brute following of instinct, and I was disgusted. I had gone so far in pursuit of a fantasy that I marvelled at it. Had anyone before me ever invested so much effort into following what was so clearly an entirely mythical dream of love? Had anyone been so blinded to common sense and the true desires of their bodies and their minds that they would invent such a get up, such a contraption as I had to fulfil an idiotic crush?

In that moment of blank awareness the bull-beast shot its fertile, bubbling seed deep inside my womb and pulled out. As it dismounted I bucked, edged away, snorted and cried. It paid me no more heed. It turned its back on me, sniffed the sea air and pawed with a certain dumb satisfaction at the sand.

Being only a woman and not a cow, I felt the vast volume of come pouring out of my tiny insides like water from a squeezed or deflating wineskin. My buttocks were slick and the upper stretches of my thighs were creamy with the semen as I felt a trickle of it leak down inside the suit. With each footstep it sank deeper and I squelched, and then something even more disheartening happened: I stopped.

Like a sudden disappointment my supernaturally endowed strength vanished, like a puff of perfume snatched away from your nose by a summer's breeze that unexpectedly changes direction. I gripped the handles inside each leg and pulled at them but they refused to budge. I shifted my legs but they too lacked the ability to set the suit moving. The complex sensation of being one with the cow-disguise evaporated too and I was just a woman helplessly pinned inside an immobile block of timber. My body became itself all by itself again and I felt the blood pumping through the narrow courses and my muscles throbbed and ached around my bones. I felt trapped, I felt claustrophobic and for a moment I almost gave way to despair and panic, but at the core of things I was still made of much sterner stuff than that.

As the tears trickled down my cheeks and the come trickled down my legs I waited for Daedalus to rescue me. Surely, I reasoned (I hoped), the bull and I had put enough distance between us for it to be safe to approach me? I couldn't see anything since my eyes were blurred with frustrated tears i couldn't wipe away but I thought or imagined there was some movement in front of me, then something unexpected happened. Once again I felt the gentle touch of the inventor on my behind, the stroke of a cloth. As he'd cleared away my husband's come in his workshop, so here out on the beach he began wiping away the bull's viscous filth.

He quickly wiped my buttocks and the upper stretched stretches of my thighs, scooped away the excessive loops of sticky semen and then he began the more delicate task of cleaning my cunt. I felt him dabbing at my distended mouth, still gaping wide open from the brutish cock that had lodged in there. With the cloth he smoothed my lips, dried them, stroked them and then to my surprise I felt his hand inside me. It slipped in easily and I could feel his fingers moving deep in me, feel the cylinder of his wrist brush gently against the walls as if it were the simplest of fits. I was shocked for a moment at the thought that this servant of the palace should think fit to fist his queen, and at a time like this, but after a few moments I came to understand, so I thought, just what the man was doing. He scooped handfuls of semen from my deepest pools and I heard them splash on the sand. Three times he plunged his hand in me – I don't know how deeply he explored, interior sensations are always magnified (simply think of the little lost tooth and the size of the gap the tongue explores), but I could have sworn I felt his elbow move at the mouth of my cunt, but I couldn't see and I never asked. He pulled out three handfuls of gunky, sticky sperm. Why he was so afraid, why the need to empty me was so urgent I couldn't grasp, though I wasn't opposed to being cleaned out. I half wished that I appreciated his deep penetration, his thick wristed fisting but I was so numbed and stretched by the bull and dazed by the sudden, clear-sighted loss of my love, that I didn't feel a single tingle of pleasure from that sanitary violation.

# viii.

Some months later it became apparent that Daedalus's attempt at post-coital cleansing wasn't so far-fetched an act as it had seemed at the time. It also turned out to not have been effective in the slightest, though I couldn't blame him for that. There's absolutely no way round the Fates when you've already been singled out.

People who should know better laugh and make crude jokes about my boy, saying how difficult, how prickly a birth it must have been for the mother (that secret has been kept, I think), but of course bulls aren't born with their horns and neither was my son. Horns come later, along with the bad tempers. As far as I knew, when I was carrying him, he was just a normal boy and was always going to be. I had no inkling that he was anything other than the king's son. I had no reason to imagine anything else – how likely was it that anyone else's seed might've taken root in my belly?

I had hoped my punishment, the king's punishment over the matter of the god's bullock, had come to an end that night on the beach, that the shame could be contained privately. But those months that passed between were simply a respite in which I could heal myself and hide myself.

The midwife was so professional that she didn't scream when she saw what emerged from me. She simply wrapped the little bundle of boy up in the clothes that lay waiting and cooed to him as she would to any baby. That too was just a respite, in-between the simple struggle of the birth (which was an easier birth than my daughter's had been) and the riot of noise that my husband would raise when he was informed of his new heir.

The calf's head perched on broad baby shoulders didn't look ugly. My boy never looked ugly, though I understand why people see him as an abomination. My husband was one of them. He shouted and railed and demanded that the doctor murder my boy. He couldn't look at me. Though he knew nothing of that night (I'd threatened Daedalus with dire warnings to keep him from speaking and I'm quite sure he didn't) he blamed me for birthing this monster, for corrupting his seed into this inhuman shape, even though I could see at the back of his face, behind that mask of indignation and hate, a patina of fear as he remembered his grandmother's meeting with the almighty Zeus and his own disrespect over the matter of the bull from the sea. The myths that wound around his life and his family had this bull motif central to them and there's little chance he couldn't have looked on this new curse in his family, this one that had poured from between my legs as a further statement of that theme. It wasn't really me he was angry at, but the universe and his appointed place in it.

I begged him not to kill the boy. He was just a harmless little innocent in all this, I pled, he had a right to live a life. But the king wouldn't hear of it, not for a long time. I wept and clutched at him as he looked away. He brushed my hands off his cloak. My cries spilt out of the palace and into the streets and I dread to think what the city thought was happening.

Eventually he gave in, to keep me quiet, let me hold my baby close to me, let me feed my son from my breast and sent for Daedalus.

Daedalus, he who's responsible for so much that happens in this palace, who initiates nothing, but who facilitates everything – from the dumb waiter that connects the kitchens and the feasting halls to the plumbing that runs water uphill to the gardens on the roof; from the semaphore towers that speak to the captains of the fleet in the harbour to the mythical, monstrous sexual couplings demanded by his employers. His eyes have seen so much that would have had him blinded, or exiled, or both, in any other kingdom, but his usefulness outweighs his dangers. He is guileless, or seems to be, an innocent, wonderful, genius fool, but I worry that one day we will let him step too far and we will see the last of him. It will either, I predict, be his death on that day or our death.

The king, my husband, explained the situation and the inventor, without a flicker of surprise, without a glimmer of memory, without a murmur of unease, set about talking of ways and schemes to keep such a boy hidden, to keep him secret, safe and secure. My husband naturally chose the most grandiose plan and within days construction work began in the vaults and catacombs to create the Labyrinth.

# ix.

Years have passed by since then. Daedalus still knows everything and still keeps quiet. The king still believes he understands everything and knows nothing. He doesn't sleep with me, believing me to have been polluted by the monster I spawned, though I don't believe he has the same disquiet about spreading his sperm around in any other open cunt he can find, even though he must still be of the impression that he fathered the boy. Chambermaids leave our service heavy with their burdens year after year – as they leave every palace, naturally. I don't care about his absence from my bed, about his unease in private with me. I am his queen and so long as the origin of the monster in the cellar is kept quiet (I believe he had the midwife murdered) then I remain in place at every feast, I am by his side meeting ambassadors and merchants and travellers from distant lands. I wear the jewellery and eat the food that befits my status. I just don't have to suffer the king's slight love-making anymore.

Besides, since that night on the beach I have been less than enthusiastic to make love. I could have any number of slaves or serving boys to fuck if I desired it, I am the queen after all, but the urge has rarely come upon me and those few times when it did I found little satisfaction in taking those tiny human members between my thighs. Far more often I've lain awake in the moonlight, listening to the waves on the beach, the slap and spray against the deceptive rocky outcrops, and have slipped my hand inside me, stroked the walls of my honey-dripping cunt with my rhythmic fingers. I pulse them in time with the sea as the faint nascent nimbus of desire for that strong, mighty bull still stirs somewhere deep in me, somewhere that should have been forgotten, that ninety-nine times out of a hundred *is* forgotten. I remember the so full sensation of his inhuman cock and the vacuum of despair as I realised that he could never love me. These twin and opposite emotions swirl like a dying maelstrom in my chest as I come, fist deep in my cunt, deep in my womb, wrist rubbing my clit, and I weep and I smile and I weep again at the difficulty of being this particular queen.

But these nights of self-pleasure (mixed in with self-loathing) are rare and far apart, and most of the time I sleep soundly, untroubled by fates or gods or destiny. I may have lost the king's love, I may never have had the bull's love, but I have one other love that sustains me and that is that love I carry in my breast and in my head for my boy.

Sometimes I creep out in the middle of the night and make my way down through the palace, down through the halls and empty passages until I reach that final set of stairs with the double-bolted doors. Then I creep down and slip through and enter the darkness of the labyrinth. Even the lamp I bring doesn't seem to spread much light in the oppressive night that lives there. Using touch as much as sight I make my way turning by turning before using the key I had Daedalus make me (no copies exist) to open shortcuts through the maze to the centre. I have trod this path so many times, from the earliest days of the construction to the present time so many years later that I can do it blindfolded, unlit, without thinking. But I need that lamp for when I reach the middle.

Then I push open the ragged curtain that separates his chamber from the mazy passageways and let the light from my lamp play across his handsome brutish features. My boy sleeps so deep, there in the depths of the night, that he has rarely even stirred at the intrusion. I'm not afraid of him: not me, not him. He's so big, so sweet sleeping there. He is so simple. The lines of his body are large, but basic, as if he's been drawn in a few thick brushstrokes. Although his body grew into a man, he never did: he's still constantly surprised at the world, at me, at himself. Every morning the day is new, the sun rises and he sees it rise above of his Labyrinth home, where Daedalus left openings and skylights, and he bellows his delight. I wish I could show him more of the world, I wish I could take my boy out, show him the world, show him to the world.

I'd like to be proud, all mothers want to be proud, but I'm not stupid or naïve enough to believe that the world wouldn't stone him and hound him and kill him, and me too, if they met him. So I take my pride, my love, in these small doses. I creep down like a burglar into his home and I watch him, like a voyeur.

Sometimes I can't help but set the lamp down by the door and climb up onto his pallet, share the prickly sticking of the straw and nestle myself up against his strong, hairy chest. Slip my neck under his arm, rest my cheek on his hot, bull neck. He's beautiful, like his father was, and I love the shape of him. The broad shoulders, the wide neck, the huge mouth and the little black eyes buried beneath the furry bony ridge of eyebrow. The smooth cold curves of his horns. Sometimes I stroke them, up above my head, as I doze in his arms. They are so hard, so proud. They're magnificent and in the moonlight are so much more impressive than the crown my husband wears – and really they are like that, they're like a crown proclaiming his dumb majesty. Because he can't talk when awake, he hasn't the throat for it and, besides, he never had the tutor for it either. As we drift together in the night I listen to his deafening breathing: hot and low and rumbling in my ear. Sometimes he grunts or roars in his sleep, in the midst of some bad dream I suspect, and I stroke his forearms with placatory gestures, firm and regular and the bellows that set my heart racing so wildly soon stop and we're both soothed by the action.

Only once did his bad dream persist. I felt his risen member behind me, human but huge, squeezed up by some nocturnal imagining against the crack of my thighs. As I stroked his arms they shifted and caught a grip on me. The one I lay above grabbed me round the chest, his great palm pressed my breast tight against me, and the other arm trailed across my belly and onto my thigh. I was pinned and he held me with such a combination of strength and finesse that I lay quite still. His unnatural hands could have crushed my ribs or wrenched my hip apart at any moment and yet he kept them just on the safe side of commanding, as if in his dream he knew exactly what he was doing.

His lower hand pulled at my dress, ripped it, tore it up above my hips, twisted my thighs apart so that I felt his hard cock pop free between them. It was hot like meat just taken from the ovens and was malleably hard; warm like bread just baked, but firm and springy like dough rising. The hand that buried itself in my crotch would not allow my thighs back together, though I struggled a little then. His finger pressed against the opening of my cunt, tugging at my hair with each clumsy movement.

Powerless in his grip he twisted us over, twisted so that I was face down in his smelly pallet of straw and he was looming large above me. The flicker of the lamp on the floor threw our big shadows across the wall like a terrifying, ugly puppet show as he grunted his hot sleepy breath down the side of my face. Resting on his elbow he was pressing me (pulling me) up against his chest. I was lifted so that with each struggle and with each breath I brushed the straw but I wasn't pushed into it. His hand clenched and unclenched on my breast, squeezing my tit as if he were a cat making itself comfortable. I knew how he was kept, what his life was like and I know that soft things, that warm things like me weren't common to him.

At the other end of me I could feel two thick fingers splaying my cunt open and the heavy meat of his great cock thumping against that gaping hole as it lolled unattended in the air. Without seeing it against my sex (though I had seen it loll before as my boy slept and even asleep it was a beautiful shaft, wrinkled and fat and brown and I had felt proud of my boy when I'd glanced at it) it felt enormous and weighty, and I hoped that he wouldn't do what it seemed he was wanting to do. At that moment I just wanted to slip out of his arms and run back to my chamber right at the top of the palace. There I'd've frigged and fisted myself silly imagining what might've happened, thinking dark and deviant thoughts in the realm of harmless fantasy away from the actual, but I couldn't get free. He was his father's son in more ways than just head and horns and impatience; there was no arguing with his muscles.

He twisted and shifted again and in a sudden blur I heard a crack from underneath us and saw something glisten white beside my eyes. It took a moment to focus and a moment longer to get the brain to focus but after those moments I recognised the slight curve and the hard sheen of one of his horns. It passed inches in front of my face and pierced the wooden boards of the pallet below us. Turning my head I

found the other horn on the other side of me – I was in a cage of two bars, but as small as it was I was unable to escape. He'd angled his head so his brow pressed into the back of my neck and his snout pointed down my spine. I could feel the damp cloud of his breath condensing there with each snuffle. His horns pointed straight down and I saw that he was using them to support the weight of his upper body.

The hand that had been pummelling my breasts skipped and jumped, literally juggling me, and moved down my belly so that it was covering my pubis mound with the fingers riding along the insides of my thighs. His other thick hand slipped out of my cunt, where it had been fumbling, and I guess it grabbed hold of his cock, because the next thing I knew I could feel the domed head of that instrument breaching the wide circle of my lips.

With one hand he held me in the air, pinned to his chest and with the other he guided his endless penis into the very place where he had begun his life. It slid and scraped in and I cried out in pain, but his half sleeping brain heard nothing and kept plunging. Time and again he fucked into me and I bit my lip and beat at the arm holding me up all to no avail. His grunting breaths came faster on my back as he slammed away and for once I grew reminiscent for the gentle, diminutive fucking of the king I had known in the old days. He may have been hard at times, he may have been thoughtless and he may have been an undiscerning fuckabout, but at least he had the good decency to lubricate, to spit or oil one's cunt before making love. But my boy hadn't had the advantages of his education and was following his own father's bestial nature. In my anger and my shame I felt, also, a sorrow for him – my poor boy.

He slipped out of me on the drawback following a particularly hard thrust and let me drop into the straw. I thought he was done, I wondered if he'd filled me with his come, whether I'd be able to slip away now. But as I brushed straw out of my eyes and tried not to breath too deeply of the stale odour that saturated his bedding I felt his hands on my hips lift my backside into the air, so my knees were dragged forward until I was practically kneeling before him. With this rearranged angle he pushed into me again, clearly not finished, clearly still as big and as hard as he'd ever been, except this time he wasn't burrowing into my cunt. That gaped unattended, open and breathy like a beached fish, as he pressed the rounded dome of his cock against the puckered, shut eye of my arsehole.

One hand gripped me round the waist tightly, so as much as I wriggled I couldn't pull free, and the other hand pointed the broad shaft into that bull's-eye opening at the base of me. I'd seen his cock, I'd felt it fill me, I'd dreamt of it, I'd tentatively touched it as he slept and I knew how thick it was, how full of life, how the pulse throbbed through it even in its most flaccid state and I knew my own limitations – I knew what I could take and what would be too much. But all the same under his insistent hammering I could feel myself giving way, with each pull away I felt a cold draught of air touching newly revealed skin.

I couldn't bear the thought of what might happen, of how long it would take to recover, if I ever could, from having that monster buried in my fundament and I fought back with all my strength. Maybe a trace of Circe's potion still remained in my system after all these years, maybe the gods were watching and felt I'd suffered enough for their fun, but however it happened I pushed away his hand and slumped on my side in his straw underneath him. He could have killed me, could've caught me easily enough, but the surprise of my escape, of my writhing free, I think must've confused his simple brain for a moment as I looked up in the lamplight to see him thrusting his cock in the empty air.

I slid to one side and rolled away, falling heavily onto the dusty stone flags of the floor. He struggled with himself, trying to stop wanking that enormous thing, at the same time as trying to pry his horns loose from the wooden slat under the straw and get himself upright to look for me. The messages coursed through his body from his sturdy brain and back again and eventually he let go of his cock and focussed on freeing himself.

I sat up on the floor and by all that would have been sane I should have run then and there, while he was still trapped, but the sight of my poor boy in such a predicament melted my heart, however bruised the rest of me was, and I stayed. I was also entranced by the sight of his abandoned prick waggling in the air between his legs as he struggled with his other horns. It was thick, long and lonely and the sack of his balls hung down comically behind it, lopsided and hairy – a thing only a mother could love without laughing.

He was having so much trouble, his weight had forced his horns so far into the wood, that I felt sure the timbers would break before he unwedged himself. I felt safe, and standing behind him I reached through his legs and with my two hands took a firm grip on his rigid thing. It was all I could do to make my hands meet their fingertips around its middle it was so big. I stroked my boy up and down his shaft, small quick movements that covered just a tiny distance of the whole and I felt a change in his demeanour. The more I manhandled that shaft the quieter he grew, the less he struggled with his horns.

It didn't take very long before he grunted, sighed and spurted his seed all over his bed and it wasn't long after that that I left an awkwardly posed, but happily sleeping boy in the middle of a labyrinth buried in a hole deep beneath my palace.

It only happened the once, that his dreams and desperations overtook him while I stole my illicit few hours being mother to my husband's shame, and it was shortly thereafter that I suggested he gift our son each year with some boys and girls purely for his amusement. My husband, the king, was owed something by the king of Athens and surely a few careless youths is a small price to ask, especially when it affords my lonely boy the chance for a little harmless amusement.

# Two: Ariadne Speaks

### i.

I'm a little confused as to what exactly happened last night. It's odd, but when I try to remember I find I split into three, or maybe four parts, and different stories fill me up. It's as if I lived that night three or four times over, each time differently, and now I've been reassembled into just one girl, unable to choose a single path for my memories to follow. And I have such a headache! Oh, it's as if I spent the darkest hours of the night sleeping in a wine butt, until the morning star rose and poured me out onto the sand and shone, far too brightly, into my eyes. And now I am awake and, so it seems, alone.

No, now I shade my eyes and look, not alone. Though the encampment has been decamped and the fires have been doused, and though the gouge of the ship's keel in the sand is even now being filled in by the endless stroking of the waves, I am being watched. There on the dunes, standing between tussock grass with his hands on his hips and the sun rising behind him is a figure I seem to recognise.

It's not Theseus, I know that. He is taller, more honed, prouder and confident. This silhouette is quite the opposite, and yet it's ringing a bell with me. As I watch it seems to shift its shape, not like someone changing positions, but like someone changing – from person to lion to serpent to ram – and yet it remains just as it is, a slightly portly, short, shy fellow. Oh, my head is spinning and it's killing me and I must sit down.

The sand is so warm, even this early in the morning and as I cast a still weary eye over the disrupted and littered beach where the camp and the Athenians were last night, I feel sleepy all over again. And as I sit there I know that the figure, the man who's watching me, has descended the dune and is walking towards me and I remember, with a start, where I saw him before.

## ii.

I was three years old when my mother went down to the beach in Daedalus's unpleasant contraption and mated with Poseidon's bull. I didn't know anything about it at the time, of course, and I didn't know anything about it for years and years later, but when I was finally told about it, finally let in on the big family secret, a lot of things that had upset my childhood fitted into place.

My father had hated me, but maybe that's a father's role. He was a king and kings always want sons and his son had been killed and he was left with me. But that's a different story. He was always busy with affairs of state and never came to my rooms and told me stories or gave me a hug, but I didn't know I was missing anything, because who misses what they know nothing of? I assumed all girls grew up in palaces with fathers who always seemed distant and uncommunicative. All the girls I knew did.

My mother on the other hand was just weird. From my earliest memory of her she was weird. She'd come and see me, when I was meant to be sleeping, she'd sneak in and sit by my bed and stroke my hair and talk to herself. This I found infuriating. It wasn't that I didn't like to be touched, to have a loving hand on me, of course I did, who doesn't like that? But she talked in a manner that is best described as low mutter. I could never make out a word, and I felt that if only I could hear what she said, then maybe I wouldn't feel as inexplicably alone as I did when she sat with me. Because, even as a very little girl, I had the sense that she wasn't really sitting with *me*, wasn't really stroking *me*.

Sometimes I'd sneak open an eye and she'd be gazing off, cheeks damp with tears, over the bed. I felt as if I was second best. I felt as if I was the cause of her tears, though I could never say why. I felt as if she hated me for some reason, and yet she sat with me and stroked my hair night after night. I feigned sleep and in time sleep came and when I'd wake in the morning there'd be my nurse hurrying me up for breakfast and for my lessons and the bright sun would banish those sad thoughts of the dark away.

The only member of the family who actually seemed to love me, was my aunt. She'd come and play with me and read to me and tell me stories of magic and monsters that would have me cowering under the furniture and then she'd whip me out by my armpits and hold me up over her head and I'd shiver and tingle as if she were sending lightning through my body. She knew all the secrets of the world, she said, and she showed me some of them, though I've long since forgotten what they were. I loved her in a way I could never love my mother, so distant and weepy and strange.

I can't remember my mother and father ever talking. But I remember my aunt smirking at them from time to time. That's the only thing I wasn't comfortable with as a little girl. Even then I wondered just what secret Circe held over them. I never thought that she was the cause of their sorrow, but she was laughing at it, whatever it was. However, like all dark things that happen to a child, in time the cloud would pass and we'd be busy collecting seashells on the beach and watching for the next ships to come sailing in from distant lands, full of strange sailors, all decked out in peculiar outfits. We'd guess the names of the lands they came from and make up stories of their adventures, because, I believed, anyone who sailed the ocean must have adventures. I certainly knew that no one who lived her life in a palace surrounded by servants and slaves would ever have one.

Did I long for adventure then? I don't know. I know I longed for a change sometimes, a chance to get away from that grim-faced woman, my mother, and that frowning urgent father of mine. And one day, when I was fifteen and feeling old and stifled and disenchanted with the entire universe, I sat in Circe's laboratory and complained.

And she sat on the edge of her desk and explained.

# iii.

I remember last night. I remember we'd beached the boat and the sailors had set the tents and started the fire and they roasted a goat they'd trapped in the hills for our dinner. I remember all that.

I was astounded that we had made it this far without being caught up with and caught. They said it was Naxos. And I knew that Naxos was far from Crete and that my father would never find me there. At least that's what I'd hoped.

I was so tired after the voyage, and I just wanted to sleep. I said as much to Theseus and he showed me to my tent. Except it wasn't just my tent, it was his too. That had surprised me a little, I'd almost forgotten why he had brought me along. I was too excited just thinking about a future away from the confines of the palace.

He lay me down on a makeshift, but comfortable, mattress and he lay down next to me. I didn't think to object, because he's not unattractive, and I had led him on somewhat.

He held my hand and stroked my hair, like someone who has found something precious and surprising and doesn't want to risk damaging it by too incautious a movement. It might be fragile, but you don't know, not until you've examined it properly, and although we'd had a certain amount of intimacy before this point, this was the first time we'd had any privacy or safety.

For such a big man his hands were surprisingly soft. They slid through my hair like the prow of his ship slid through the wave crests and I shut my eyes. I was feeling very sleepy and he wasn't helping to keep me awake.

But then the hand of his that had been holding mine let go and I felt the fingertips begin touching a raindrop pattern of taps on my thigh. My dress had ridden up a little and the fluttering, ethereal brushing of his fingers on my bare skin was delicious. So close to tickling that it woke me up; so close to pleasure that it made me shiver.

As he saw me stretch and smile he became more confident with me, he regained some of that authoritative swagger he had outside with his men. He played his fingers in fugue-like intricacies of pitter-patters across my inner thigh, steadily heading north from my knee, though so slowly that I was quite convinced he'd never reach that little mouth that had woken up with me.

Long before he reached it he leant over and kissed me. It was a loving kiss, long and deep and I hurt from the prickle of his stubble but at the same time I revelled in the masculine imposition of it. I felt for a moment like a helpless princess rescued from some dark fate, as if he were my handsome prince come to whisk me away to a happy ever after ending, though I knew the truth was more complex than that. But that's how I felt for a moment lying beside his strong body, knowing that he could crush me in his hands the way he had killed my brother... my half-brother. Even as I thought about that monster I recognised a resemblance between the two of them: no matter how much revulsion I felt at the sight or the thought of that half-human animal, I could see the reflection of his pure strength and his unthinking virility in this new lover of mine.

Theseus' tongue grappled with mine and I pressed my face up to mash our lips together, to clash teeth and to engulf him as well as I could with my sudden gush of desire. He lent his weight on me, pushing me back down to the bed and with his spare hand he clutched the back of my neck and bent me so my mouth raised and opened of its own accord. His fingers were strong and dug into the muscles that laced the nape of my neck, dug into them and relaxed them and another shiver rippled through my body. I shut my eyes, lay back, focussed on his fingers, his mouth, the sheer stony weight of him squashing me down. I was small, powerless and puffy with desire as he kissed my arched, exposed throat.

I sighed powerfully, unable to draw enough breath into me, as his lower fingers finally finished their interminable march north. Still fluttering, still annoyingly slight in their touch, still an irritating, teasing counterpoint to the hardness of his kisses, they finally, eventually, brushed against what lay between my parted thighs. I'd opened my legs to him as I'd opened my mouth to him.

We'd run so far and so fast; since he'd performed his awful deed in the darkness of the Labyrinth we'd been running, we'd been praying for the right winds, urging the sailors to row harder, watching the horizon for sign of pursuit. After all that time, a time in which boredom had soon mixed with the ebbing thrill of adventure and infraction, I realised, lying in that bed with that man, that all I was seeking was a release for the tension that I hadn't realised had built up in me. Here I was, miles from home, untraceable, unfindable, free from the dreariness of my parents and their bizarre, unnatural world and finally I was really, really free.

I wrapped my arms around Theseus' back and pulled him closer to me (though there was barely any closer he might come, he was lying in such weighty proximity), and dug my fingers into his spine as his, blunter, fingers were still kneading my neck.

I willed the lips of my secret mouth to open wider, to suck his searching fingers in, and in my imagination they moved, they called out to him like a siren and they caught hold of those skipping, tickling fingers. They held them tight, as slick and frictionless as those little wings were, and I felt the outline of each distinct fingertip trace a different course across my little mouth. He stroked lovingly, but firmly; touchingly, but with fervour. He explored for himself I think, finding my shape, finding my proportions and then finding my sweet pearl of joy.

I shuddered enough that he was dislodged from my mouth, from his fervered kisses, and I laughed at him as he looked curiously in the half light, a brief worry crossing his face, but I assured him, without words, but with a firm guiding hand, that he had been right to touch me there. I positioned his hand softly, on top of the singularity and showed him how to brush across it, from side to side, so softly that the outer limit of his flesh almost didn't touch the tip of my lovely spot. Just the slightest of brushes, that's how I like it, and that's how I taught him as we lay there, now side by side and he entered into the sport. Sometimes all I felt was the passage of air and he whisked through the damp curling hair, and sometimes he'd bang clumsily and make me cry out and jerk. But mostly he had it just right and with speed and stamina to go forever it seemed.

I drifted, happily half-dozing in a bubble of pleasure that levitated me from the bed, from my old life and I dreamt of the whole open future before me. A new world.

But then, either he grew tired or he grew bored, or maybe both, because he drew his hand away, lent over and kissed me again, slipping his tongue deep behind my teeth, just as he slipped his upstanding piece deep into my secret place.

I was so loose and so relaxed and so wet from his previous ministrations and from my pleasant drowsy dreams that he shot all the way in, filling me right up and taking me by surprise. I could feel his hairy thighs pushing my thighs even further apart, I could feel his heavy marbles bang against my buttocks and his stomach pressed down on mine. This pressure relaxed as he drew his golden member out, right to the tip so that I felt for a moment as if I were being left, but he remained with me, though barely.

He was lent up on his elbows and we were just linked by both my mouths. So slightly. Our lips touched above and he flicked his tongue across my teeth as I sighed into him; below my lips were slickly kissing the very head, the very crown of his piece. He felt like such a saviour in that moment I regretted having used him so. But such thoughts were only fleeting and shadowy in my mind and I wanted him to plunge back into me, to fill me back up, to reverse the gape I felt inside, or better to drive himself slowly in, like a farmer behind his oxen who has only a short field left to plough but all afternoon in which to do it. I wanted him to make love gently, lovingly – I liked the feeling I got from thinking he was in love with me, that I was loved (it was quite sweet really) – but I also wanted him to ravage me, to think nothing of me and to take me firmly, boldly and rapidly.

Oh, my mind was confused and spinning through all sorts of imaginings right then, and indeed he did plunge his member back in, slamming his hips into my thighs, pushing my legs still further apart. I felt the breeze cooling against my perspiring skin. I almost loved him for it. I scratched my nails into his back, kissed him hungrily, sucking on his tongue, as he pumped away inside me like a relentless piston. I thought

of Daedalus's workshop and young Icarus, and then he upped the speed.

With each inner thrust I squeezed him tight, and the air came gasping, thumping out of my lungs. It seemed he was driving the very spirit out of me. I let go his mouth, let go his back and just lay there, a helpless toy, and let him pump and pump as the thrills accumulated throughout my belly, the little buzz and hum of an approaching peak, seen someway off, but I knew that progress toward it was steady. And as it grew closer I could see it was a big summit, a broad plateau set atop a high slope and I was being propelled up that steep hillside, that mountainside.

And then, astounded that it could appear and arrive in such sweet, swift succession, I was there, mindless and shivering, a cold glow spurting down my spine, connecting all parts of me together and to the gods. And my eyes were shut and my mouth was open and my ears thumped with blood, and when I came to I found that Theseus had rolled off and was already snoring and there was a sticky pool of his residue on my belly, dribbling sadly down one side, and I felt empty, and emptied. There was a gap between my legs, which though numb was still making its awareness known.

I climbed up from the bed and pulled my robe around me. I walked on unsteady legs (it had been a pleasant battering I'd succumbed to) out into the quiet night and I saw the stars circling overhead and the faintest nimbus of dawn striking the eastern sky and the clink and snore of the camp filled the beach.

I walked up into the dunes to pee and did so, and then I found somewhere soft to lie for a while and look at the sky. So beautiful, I thought looking at the stars and the nebulae.

How I loved this sight, how I loved the freedom to watch it in the dark, by myself, and think of what else was happening in the world, so far away, all the turmoil and tribulation. How my crazy mother might be coping with her newfound loss. Gods, I didn't mind not being there for that. Just me and the stars, and then I fell asleep.

And now here I am, almost alone on the empty beach, confused about what happened last night.

# iv.

I was fifteen when Circe finally told me why things were so weird.

'You know about the Minotaur in the cellar?' she'd said.

I'd told her I had, because obviously we all knew about that. It was one of the things, I'd been taught, that made Crete great, that gave us power over other nations. It was a blessing from the gods.

'Well, that's your brother.'

Naturally I didn't understand what she meant and I said so.

She went on and explained, in the face of my several and varied vocal protests, just how my mother had given birth to this monster because she'd mated with a bull. It all seemed, not only a bit far-fetched, but also no way to talk about the royal family. If Circe hadn't been the woman she was, and my mother's sister at that, I'd've called for a guard right then and there, however little I liked my mother. Even then I wondered if Circe wasn't just feeling sour grapes because Pasiphae had married a king and she hadn't, and was talking slander out of spite.

I simply couldn't believe that anyone would make love to an animal like a bull, I mean, outside of fairytales, who'd ever heard of such a ludicrous thing? But Circe told me to go and speak to Daedalus if I didn't believe her.

So I walked the miles of corridor down to his dark workshop, so similar in many ways to Circe's laboratories, except less musty. His place smelt more of oil and metal and sand, whereas hers was dusty and organic and smelt of herbs and things that had been herbs but which now were rotting in a pestle or in a corner. I think hers was the more scary of the two, though I'd never really noticed that as a child.

I found Daedalus pottering at a desk with an eyeglass squeezed into one eye and pair of tiny tweezers moving some piece of miniscule machinery around. Without waiting for him to notice me or to say 'good morning' I asked him straight out about my mother.

'Did you help my mother make love to a bull?' I asked.

He flustered and dropped the tweezers and swore and took the eyeglass out of his eye and turned around to look at me. He stroked his beard and gathered himself up before answering.

'Ah, Princess Ariadne,' he said, 'Whatever are you talking about?'

'My mother,' I said.

'And a bull?' he said.

'Yes,' I said. 'I heard,' I added, 'That you helped her to have sex with a bull once. Is it true?'

He looked at the ceiling and tugged at his beard and looked to be calculating something under his breath, which was, all in all, a fairly normal moment in a conversation with Daedalus (he wasn't one to focus too well on other people, I knew that). 'Hmm,' he said after a moment, 'No, of course I didn't do something like that, it would have been... oh, what's that word? Um, immoral, wouldn't it, to copulate with Poseidon's own bull... what a terrifying thought. No, Princess, nothing like that ever happened.'

Then, as if the conversation were at an end he turned and sank to his knees to look for something on the floor under his desk and started humming to himself tunelessly.

I felt frustrated. I didn't know whether I believed him or

not, I didn't know whether I believed Circe or not. I mean I knew she had a perverted sense of humour sometimes, turning the slaves into all sorts of animals for her own amusement and the like. Or so I'd heard. I wanted to ask Daedalus again, thinking maybe he'd forget what he just told me and tell me a different story this time, but I knew he wasn't fool enough to contradict himself straight away, and besides, did I really want to catch him in a lie – he who'd made me such marvellous toys and dolls as a little girl? Although I'd long since grown out of love for those little figures that moved about by themselves and which cried and needed picking up in the night, I still remembered them fondly. No, I couldn't force this old man to tell me any more, I didn't want to catch him in a lie, so I turned and left the workshop.

As I stepped outside the doorway a hand touched my shoulder and I almost leapt out of my skin. I don't think I yelped, but it was so unexpected that I was more shocked than I should've been.

To my surprise it was Icarus. He was Daedalus's boy, his son, and was ten years or so older than me. I'd seen him on occasion and always thought he was quite nice. He had a pleasant grin and was always quietly fiddling with things when his father was displaying some new gadget or device to the court. Icarus would be there tinkering with a few last cogs and screws. Sometimes he'd get down on his knees to peer underneath the contraption (Daedalus had a bad back, he said, which meant he couldn't bend over so much) and I remember more than once staring at his hips and thighs and backside as he did so. They'd filled me on those few occasions with a delightful, if troubling, itch which only went away when I was left alone in my room at the end of the day.

'I heard what you were asking,' he said to me, in a whisper, 'Come back tonight and I'll show you something interesting... your highness.'

And then his hand was off my shoulder and he was lightly skipping back into the workshop and talking to his father in a loud voice and I was left alone in the dark hallway, wondering just what I ought to do. Well, I knew there was only one thing to do and that was what I did.

Later that day, when the lamps had been extinguished and the sun and the moon had both set leaving just the silvery haze of starlight above the palace I took up a lamp of my own and tiptoed down through the Labyrinth of the palace that sat atop the other, more mythic, labyrinth beneath the palace, and down that last corridor that led to Daedalus' workshop.

There was a light on in it and I waited just outside the door for a moment before peering round it. I worried that maybe Daedalus would be there, but all I could see was dark-headed Icarus sat up on one of the benches reading a scroll.

He glanced over at me, though I was sure I hadn't made a sound, and gestured for me to come in.

I did so.

Without saying a word he took my hand and walked me through several doors into another room much like the first workshop, where there were old experiments and devices lying around. Some were covered with sheets, some were broken and leant against the wall. I recognised a few bits and pieces – there was a mechanical band that had played at a party the year before, and there was a sort of oven I remembered him displaying once to the king that took sand and turned it into bricks, but bricks which you could see through. Some of his things had worked and some had sort of worked, and some had done nothing at all. But my father seemed to like the man, even amid his failures.

Icarus pulled me over to a far corner where something huge lurked under a dust sheet. I didn't know what it was and even after he tugged the fabric out of the way I wasn't sure at first. It looked like a statue of a cow, made of wood, perhaps, and patchily covered up with real hides.

It didn't look very realistic.

Icarus pulled himself up one of the thing's flanks and unhooked a catch which let the whole top of the animal open up.

'Look,' he said, 'She'd lie in here and then...'

I still didn't quite see.

He jumped down and pulled a little ladder out from somewhere and urged me to climb up it. When I reached the top I looked in and saw that there was indeed room in the cow to lie down, to fit your arms and legs, it seemed, into the cow's legs and there was a hole in the end through which I could see the yellow glow of the lamp. It was an oval hole and when I realised what it revealed, what part of my mother's anatomy would be displayed through it I blushed deeply and lost the ability to speak.

I wanted to ask Icarus how it had worked, whether she'd really climbed inside this thing. If she had then surely that meant that what Circe had told me was true. I think I was crying as these thoughts tumbled through me. I hadn't really wanted to believe something so vile about my mother, had I? No, even though she was distant and unhappy, I hadn't wanted to believe that some bizarre secret shame like this might be behind it. Why not something simple like a stillborn son or an affair with a man?

I was in shock as the truth of everything tumbled into me

and I hardly noticed as Icarus encouraged me to step into the cow. I think I thought that he wanted me to understand what my mother had felt, that he was trying to give me some little insight into why she had done the extreme, bizarre things she had done. But now, after the event, I know he had other things on his mind. I suspect, in fact, that he had planned this all along (well, not all along – not from the building of the cow, but from that afternoon at least), because as soon as my two legs slid down the smooth gullies inside the cow's legs, and I was struck, unable to climb out without help, he suddenly sprang into action and pushed me forwards so that I was lying down and the next thing I knew was that the roof of the cow was shut down on top of me.

My arms were pinned to my sides and it was only a reflex that had turned my face up to look out along the cow's neck that had given me access to breathable air. But I knew what my mother had felt, because my legs were being pulled so far apart – the cow was built in such a way as to accentuate that gap. I felt my hidden places were on display, were tearing open, but I knew that the tail of my tunic was still covering me, because I could feel it.

But then that wretched boy slid down from the side of the cow and crept round to the back and lifted it up. I felt him do it and I shouted and writhed and cried out at him. This was no way at all to treat a princess, I thought. I called him every name I could think of, all of them highly unsavoury, but that piece of cloth wasn't replaced and I knew he could see my secret mouth, with its thin hair and its little lips pouting upright like some slave girl. Oh, I felt angry more than anything, and then I stopped feeling angry and gave into something else – or rather I continued feeling angry, but for a moment was distracted.

I think it must have been his tongue, in fact now I know it was his tongue, because I felt it again afterwards a number of times, in less constrictive situations. But he lapped up and down my little breathless opening in a way I had never felt before and it was like having a liquid of joy poured on me. As if the nectar that only the gods can drink were being dripped, drop by drop, across that little mouth and it had the effect of invigorating and expanding and satisfying and warming as much there as it would have were you to swallow it. Oh, it felt good and he kept licking, right from my little nub of pleasure between my pink-lipped lips to the open air.

I couldn't move. I couldn't fight back. I couldn't resist. For appearance sake I protested whenever I remembered to, but more often I remembered what I'd thought about this man when I'd watched him down on his knees tinkering underneath some machine or other, how I'd wished to have lifted up his tunic and kissed his soft, stretched buttocks, and how I'd imagined in deepest secrecy what he might be like were he to visit my bed. When alone, sometimes, I'd touched myself in the very place from which he was now drinking.

But I was the princess, and he was just the palace nut's son, so I struggled and shouted a bit more.

Perhaps to quiet me down, perhaps for reasons of his own, perhaps for no reason at all, I felt him slip a fingertip through that wettest of channels and then plunge the slick tip into me. Not where I most secretly wanted him to stick it, but into my little bottom. He didn't dig far, but he hooked it and jiggled it and at the same time he mouthed steadily on my little pleasure point. On and on went these twin sensations, as if he were tireless, until I couldn't stand it anymore and I climaxed inside that cow, immobile and unable to stop him from continuing, pushing me over a second peak and spraying his face with juice like an overripe fruit.

Eventually he unlocked me, and helped me to climb out, since I was somewhat unsteady on my feet.

I pulled my tunic back down, back into place and gave him a stern look.

He grinned like the naughty schoolboy who'd got the cream.

I tried a haughty look and then I tried a scowl, but none of it really seemed to work.

He pulled a key from his belt and handed it to me.

'This,' he said, as if nothing out of the ordinary had happened at all, 'Opens secret doors in the labyrinth.' He told me how my mother sometimes followed the hidden route to visit the beast in the centre. I could follow her if I still didn't believe the whole of the story.

After being in the cow, after being so well treated, I'd almost forgotten why I was there. But I took the key and said a swift goodnight to Icarus, without blushing very much and without displaying any tenderness at all, I walked quickly back up through the palace.

I did follow her, another night, and I saw that Circe was right about everything, as usual.

## V.

I remember last night. I remember we'd beached the boat and the sailors had set the tents and started the fire and they roasted a goat they'd trapped in the hills for our dinner. I remember all that.

I was astounded that we had made it this far without being caught up with and caught. They said it was Naxos. And I knew that Naxos was far from Crete and that my father would never find me there. At least that's what I'd hoped.

We were all tired after having come so far so fast, but the Athenians were also eager to celebrate their victory and their survival. They pulled out instruments – a beautiful tortoiseshell lyre, some drums and pipes – and some of the women, so recently under sentence of death in the Minotaur's lair, danced in the flickering light of the camp fire. If I hadn't been sitting with Theseus and sharing his plate I might've got up myself, but these women knew different dances to any I had seen at home in Crete and they all knew one another – I was just the strange girl who'd been picked up to them. They didn't even look at me much. The men, however, paid more attention. I think they were jealous that I was on Theseus's arm and not theirs.

But then in the middle of the dancing and feasting a cry came up from one of the men. He was outside the firelight and we couldn't see him, but all the men jumped to their feet when they heard it, dropping their instruments and stilling the evening air.

At first it had sounded as if the cry had been of pain or terror, the way it echoed above the music, but in the silence of the camp it was clear it had a different cause – it was a cry of joy.

An excited fellow ran into the firelight, into one of the sailor's arms and pointed back out into the night.

'Wine!' he shouted excitedly, 'Come, look, there's wine here...'

This strange exclamation required some explanation and when he'd got his breath back he explained how he'd been off to answer a call of nature and out in the dark of the beach he'd tripped over something. When he'd looked closely he'd found it was an amphora and when he'd looked even closer he discovered there was a whole stash of them, half buried on the beach. Cracking the seal on one of them he dipped his finger in and tasted it, sourly expecting it to be oil, but discovering against all hope a lovely rich heady wine.

As the men went off to drag this surprise hoard back to the camp they argued among themselves as to how they'd managed to miss the jars during the afternoon when they landed. Some suggested the waves must've uncovered some merchant's store or a smuggler's hidden booty, while others claimed it must be a gift from the gods to celebrate their escape from Crete. Either way they didn't worry too much or for too long about it.

The jars were opened and drinks poured for everyone, even the women, and the celebrations began again. The music, however, lasted only a short while, as rapid, untempered drinking (fresh water was in even shorter supply than the wine was) led to a sleepiness that laid low first the dancers, then the musicians, then even Theseus himself, who slumped to the ground with his head in my lap, quietly snoring away. Strangely, only I seemed to remain awake, even though I'd drained my cups like all the rest

I sat for a while listening to the cicadas, the sleepers and the waves and watching the writhing flames of the bonfire before I became aware of somebody sitting beside me.

When I looked I found that a warm faced, round-nosed gentleman had joined me. He was in his forties, perhaps, and his eyes sparkled coolly, even as the orange glow of the fire played across them. There was something about them that was held steady, even as he hiccoughed.

'I'm sorry,' he said, leaning toward me and resting a hand on my shoulder, 'I'm a little the worse for wear tonight. I've been drinking.' At this he gestured all around him, as if to point to all the others who had rolled themselves up in their blankets, or who had simply passed out where they'd been sat.

'Me too,' I said, not feeling the slightest bit tipsy.

I didn't recognise him from the ship, and I wondered if maybe this area of the island wasn't as uninhabited as we'd thought. Maybe it had been his wine we'd dug up and drunk, and now he wanted to make some complaint? But he smiled slowly at me with those grey-blue eyes and didn't seem the least upset by all the inebriated sleepers.

'Was it yours?' I asked.

'Oh, yes, I'm afraid so,' he chuckled tipsily. He seemed to be embarrassed to admit it, as if he were embarrassed to admit that we'd done him the disservice of stealing a dozen or so of his amphorae, or as if he didn't much care, or thought it a joke.

'I'm sorry,' I blustered, meaning to speak for everyone.

He smiled again and moved his hand from my shoulder, where it had rested on the clasp of my tunic, to touch my neck.

I wasn't sure what to say. Theseus was still snoring in my

lap and this strange old stranger was stroking, very pleasantly, along the artery that pulsed in my throat.

For some reason I didn't move away, though I did look away.

I suspected that maybe this viticulturist was going to exact payment for the theft of his wine in the only way men tend to think of extracting payment from women. But at the same time as thinking this other thoughts came into my head, such as the vague memory of being taught somewhere, sometime, to always be gracious to strangers because you'll never know when one of them might be a god in disguise. It was a strange thought to pop unannounced into my mind, but it stayed with me for a moment and I remember smiling at him as I thought it.

His fingers were soft and warm in the cool of the night and they stroked so gently that I didn't want to move away.

This is nice, I thought to myself, but I'll stop him if he tries anything else – I'll wake Theseus and he can deal with this old man.

But when he reached my earlobe and teased it and stroked it between his finger and thumb and then circumnavigated the whole of my stiff little auricle I did nothing. It was as if I were stuck there and the movements of his fingers connected with nerves which connected directly into my brain. It was as if I were being tickled inside my head – in a most delicious way. It was like a moving itch, a self-conscious itch that was able to always keep just out of reach of the scratch that came along following it.

Then he stroked my hair, slowly and gently, and leant over and put his tongue in my ear.

I hadn't been expecting that and I jumped, not because it was unpleasant, but because I knew where I was drawing the line. A little petting, a little stroking – that's acceptable under the extraordinary circumstances we found ourselves in; but kissing my ear like that, was quite out of the question.

I would've slapped him and even raised my hand in order to do so when I looked once again in his eyes. Although his face and his body were those of a man of middle-age, his eyes seemed so much younger, sparkling and limpid. And as I looked at them I thought, why protest? I thought, my lover is asleep and the night is young, and besides this fellow doesn't look all that bad, especially not for someone his age, and after all we did drink his wine...

These thoughts tumbled one after another through my brain without me expecting them, and he smiled again, that innocent, cheeky, lovely smile of his and I moved the hand that was still in the air, which had been aiming a slap, and touched the side of his face, stroked his curly beard and brushed his ear.

'You're right, of course,' he said mysteriously.

And then he lent over and kissed me.

Oh, I hadn't been expecting that, I thought, and even more surprising to me was the fact that I kissed him back.

His mouth tasted like the rich purple wine we'd drunk earlier, as if he too had been sipping it all night. Our tongues touch-tipped and then we parted to take some fresh air.

I felt quite light-headed then, in exactly the same way that I hadn't earlier on.

I hiccoughed nervously and then laughed.

He kissed me again, running his fingers through my hair and I held onto Theseus's head in my lap, as if it were some sort of security, something solid keeping me at a fixed point in space. The rest of me drifted in the kiss, in the stroking, and when I felt his hand unhook my tunic at the shoulders and let the cloth fall to reveal my breasts, I didn't move a muscle.

He broke off from the kiss then. Lent back, still holding my head, just as I held Theseus's, and he looked at me, staring into my eyes and at the same time roving across my body. He smiled his fixed, lopsided, slightly off-kilter smile still, and I could tell he meant it.

I let go of Theseus and the world span for a moment, as if standing up drunk, but I raised my hands to my breasts and lifted them for him, showing them off. My nipples were brown and flat and stared at him like eyes too tired to open wide, but astonishingly intrigued all the same.

He lent down and sucked one then the other and the string inside me that connects those buttons to the one in-between my legs spontaneously caught fire. It was like a channel of oil, spilt and set alight – the flame spreads seamlessly across the surface, burning brightly and all over, a straight line into the distance – in this case a direct line to my most sensitive spots. I wondered if Theseus might wake up soon, smelling the rising ripe scent of that secret, damp forest down there. But he didn't shift and this stranger continued to suck me, always moving from one to the other just in time, just as I began to feel too wildly unbalanced. I breathed deep gulps of the cool night air, in the hope that they might clear my head, but it had no effect and in fact I now found myself feeling more and more light-headed every minute that the evening went on.

When he finally let go of me, when he once again lent back and roved my half naked body with his eyes, I held my breasts up and waved them at him again. I didn't want to be left, to be abandoned like that, not right then. They had more sucking left in them, they weren't quite numb yet, not entirely. I was like a petulant brat, angry that she'd been told enough was indeed enough, demanding just one more go.

As I waved them I noticed that they were wet, naturally with his spit, where he'd drooled over them (I'd felt it dripping down my belly as he'd sucked away), but when I looked down I saw in the starlight that they were dark with moisture and raising my hand to my nose I smelt that it was yet more wine.

As I dried my breasts with my tunic I saw that the wine was leaking out of me, out of the tiny pinhole pricks which should, in later life, have produced milk. Instead, here, on this strange beach, I was bleeding wine. If it had happened any other day of my life I would have freaked out, I would have leapt to my feet and shrieked, but last night I just stared at it numbly and dumbly – more interested than shocked. It was funny and I laughed, just as he laughed.

After a minute or two the flow of wine stopped, but not before I'd mischeviously dripped a few drops into Theseus' open, snoring mouth, which gaped ominously in my lap, just as my own other little mouth gaped underneath him.

My new friend with the amazing tongue stood up. He tottered to his feet and wobbled in front of me. I was feeling so unashamed at it all that I simply stared at the front of his tunic where his manhood was lifting it up and I knew that I wanted to see it.

So I just reached out and drew back the cloth and revealed his purple headed thing, all stiff and handsome and I popped my lips over the end of it and sucked, just as he had sucked on my breasts minutes before. It seemed only fair really, to repay one good deed with another.

He groaned and moaned and hiccoughed above me and I giggled and licked and sucked down below, and Theseus snored in my lap.

The whole thing was quite ridiculous really. Why I didn't

wonder to myself how it was that no one had woken up, or why I was doing what I was doing, I don't know. I wonder now, sat on this beach all by myself. I look back at the things I've done and I marvel and blush, but last night, I didn't question anything, my head was so filled with the vine.

After an age of sucking he stepped back, pulled himself from my mouth and took hold of his hardness by the base.

'Open up,' he said, hiccoughing, but still with a certain air of authority.

I knew this game because Icarus had done it once and I wasn't going to start objecting to things now, so I just lent back on my hands and opened my mouth.

His big thing wobbled before me and he jerked his body and then he shot his load right into my mouth, but instead of the sour prickle I was expecting, it was yet more wine. The night was suspended in it – the world seemed to have become a giant amphora with all of us dangling in it, stuck, floating inside of it.

Heady purple wine, and not just a few blobs of it like Icarus had fed me, but a stream that kept pouring. My mouth filled faster than I could swallow and the strong smelling juice poured out the corners of my mouth and ran down my neck in trickling, tickling, streams. I closed my mouth and wine gushed like waterfalls and my breasts felt the warm caress as rivers poured into my tunic, which was growing utterly sodden. Each stream splashed up into Theseus' hair and a few expectorations of mine splashed on his face – but still he didn't shiver or turn or show any signs of waking.

My man aimed his purple stream across my breasts, beating my nipples, cowering them down with the pressure as they popped up and he lifted his penis and squirted his juice in my hair and across my face and all I could do was gulp for air and laugh and drink as much of him down as I could, until eventually I can remember no more.

At some point I must have passed out and then, when I woke, the next morning or perhaps the one after that, the Athenians had gone. Maybe I'd been lost somehow, maybe I'd wandered off in the night and they'd searched for me. Maybe they found me wine splattered and shattered and they just didn't want to take me with them and they crept away. I don't know. I really don't know.

And so now here I am, almost alone on the empty beach, confused about what happened last night.

## vi.

After I'd learnt the truth of my mother's bizarre secrets I must admit I purposefully became a worse and worse daughter. I don't know if she ever knew that I knew, because I never said it to her face – the opportunity never arose, since she and I were alone together so little, and it wasn't an opportunity I'd ever have grasped anyway – but every time I saw her it seethed round in the middle of my stomach like a snake or a worm that was growing hungry. It was abysmal.

I couldn't understand how she could have done anything like that, couldn't understand what would drive a woman to abandon her husband and daughter for such a monstrous deed: weren't we family enough, weren't we enough to love? Oh, it was all too much to think about and stay sane and so I did what any good daughter would do in the circumstances, which was to rebel. And I think now, sat on this far off beach, that if I hadn't done that, if I'd remained quiet and nursed my revulsion all by myself then I might still be in the palace, waited on by servants and dressed in fine gowns.

At first I hated Icarus as much as I hated my parents. After all he was the one who had finally pulled the wool away from my eyes. I tried to keep away from him and whenever we happened to find ourselves in the same room I firmly and determinedly looked elsewhere.

I'd gone to see Circe, to cry on her shoulder about everything that was making me feel sick, but she'd changed. She laughed, and it wasn't comforting. I saw in a flash that she'd only ever been a troublemaker. She had no life of her own, no love of her own, no interests outside meddling in the lives of others – in making their lives a mess. I wouldn't be surprised if she didn't have something to do with persuading father to keep that bull from the sea in the first place. She says one thing, always, and behind it lurks a whole row of other effects waiting to be caused. She's evil, wicked and quite, quite sad.

But I didn't have that objectiveness a few years ago, and when she first scorned my tears I ran from her chambers not understanding how she could reject me so, after so many years of being my only and best friend. I ran through corridor after corridor back to my own rooms and pushing my maid aside I threw myself down on my bed and wept, wept, wept.

I was so alone in the world. I'd look out my window or stand on my balcony and I could see the sea. I could watch the ships sailing and I remembered how Circe and I used to watch them and a stone hung from my heart, but I also saw how they sailed away from this place, off toward the horizon where anything could happen, where everything new began. Those ships, I knew were free in a way I would never be so long as I stayed there. But I didn't really believe I'd ever get to leave, after all that palace was, more or less, all the world I knew.

Sometime later – oh, months went by in my misery – I bumped into Icarus again. I was wandering the passages late in the night, unable to sleep, and I think he had been doing the same. He was still the handsome young man I had thought about many times in my narrow bed, and I blushed as I remembered what had happened the last time we'd actually met, that night when he'd broken the truth open for me. Fortunately in the lamplight he wouldn't have been able to see that blush.

He asked me what I was doing up so late, so far from the

royal quarters, and like a dam that has been untended for decades I suddenly burst open and told him everything. We talked for hours – or rather I talked for hours and he listened – round and round the subjects. There really was quite little to actually say, but he listened to my complaints in every variation I could think of and he put his arm around me and rested my head on his breast, even as we sat there in the dust of some distant corridor. He smoothed my hair and soothed my tears and eventually silence came to us.

After that I met him again and again. Night after night we would meet in secret out of the way places and we would make love. It was my own way, I see now, of defying my parents, because I had no other way to do so, other than suicide, and I never really thought of something as drastic as that. I may have been angry, I may have been mad, but I knew that all the chance for any sort of fun or happiness in this world ends when you go underground.

Though, that said, on some nights we would go as deep underground as we dared, following the secret safe paths through the Labyrinth to gaze through the doorway at the slumbering Minotaur. He was such an ugly brute, so thick limbed and all asthmatic and unhappy. I felt revolted, I felt sick every time I saw the monster, but we'd stand there in that doorway and my boy Icarus would lift the back of my tunic up and slip his lovely thing between my legs and in front of that terrible deviation from all that is good and holy we would pleasure ourselves: he would rub that stiff piece of man along the lips of my slick little mouth, sending shivers all through me, in all directions, and I'd reach down and hold him against me firmly and press the head against my little flickering button and all the time I'd be fixed on the monster in the straw bed in front of us.

I knew if ever it woke up it could kill us both, of course it could. Its muscles rippled like snakes under the flesh as it shifted from time to time in its sleep. And it would grunt. Its thick bull lips would drip with spittle and it would fart all through the night. And as I looked at this vision, my lover, my dear Icarus, would whisper in my ear the truth of my relationship with the bull-man – it was my brother, and I would feel more and more nauseous, even as the wonder of my little joy approached.

Oh, we did other things too, Icarus and I. We did everything. He taught me everything. He was the first man I took in my mouth, or anywhere. He would sometimes find me wandering in the palace during the day, on my way to this or that meeting, and would apologise to my companions, saying that he had to pass a message on to me and I would tell them to go on and that I'd catch them up and he'd drag me round the corner, just out of sight but probably still in earshot and urge me to my knees, pull out his sweet tool and have me kiss the end of it. Sometimes it would just be a stolen moment before I had to run back, but sometimes it would be enough time to make him spill his pale seed in the dust. He was so beautiful when he did that. His little eyes would roll up and his face would go red and his mouth open without making a noise. I smiled because it was I who was doing such things to him.

He taught me to make love. He came to my bed more than once, where I had imagined him as a girl. Sometimes I went to his. At other times we met in the open air or in public places. Those few years we stole from out of the teeth of time and fate were such fun, I shall never forget them, not one moment of them for as long as I live.

One night he led me by the hand back to the workshop

where we had first been intimate and he had me strip my clothes. This wasn't unusual, but I still got a thrill in my stomach from standing naked before him, especially in such a workaday place as this, surrounding by the benches where I'd seen his father tinkering so often, and especially with him still all covered up. I stood with my hands on my hips and with my feet apart and asked him what he wanted to do. The buzz in-between my legs had begun and my little nipples were standing up pointing at him and I knew what I hoped he wanted to do. It had been some weeks since I had seen him – he'd claimed to have been working on an important project of some sort with Daedalus, and as far as I knew he had been. This hiatus hadn't made me sad, because our relationship had always been stolen when we could and gaps of work or duty or inconvenience were built into it, but it had made me hungry.

This night he held up before me some sort of machine, telling me it was a present, something he'd made just for me. I do believe he was fully as brilliant as his father was when it came to making things and having the ideas, except where Daedalus was absent-minded and eclectic in his designs, Icarus was focussed and his creations tended to be firmly of one particular bent.

What he held up was shaped a bit like a mechanical crab, though it only seemed to have five legs – four narrow ones protruding from each corner, and one thicker one jutting from the centre of its squat little body.

But, of course, when he brought it closer I realised that that fifth protuberance wasn't a leg at all, or if it was then it had become highly specialised for some other task. It was shaped just like a male member, and in fact I suspect Icarus had modelled it on himself – naturally it was a little bigger and a little thicker than his lovely tool, but that just convinces me all the more of it – I'm sure men always see their things that way.

Icarus led me to one of the workbenches he had cleared of rubbish and bid me lie down. He had laid out a couple of blankets to make it not quite so hard and I climbed up quite happily.

As I lay back with my knees up and my legs swaying slightly apart I waited. It normally didn't take Icarus very long at all before he would jump on me and kiss and lick me – oh, the boy was smitten with me something dreadful! (Boy! He was so much older than me, but all the same he was like a child with a new present when we were together – he was always excited about having me, even when he acted so cool and blasé. I had to laugh sometimes and he'd ask me what I was laughing at and if ever I told him it was him he'd get all sullen and grumpy, as if I had insulted his lovely, smooth manhood – but I was just laughing with the joy of it, at the fact that I, simply through my existing and acquiescing, could lighten the world in quite this way. I had to laugh – me who was silent and sullen myself around everyone else, came so alive and so infectiously so, when he touched me, either in my body or in my thoughts.)

I lay there on the workbench expecting him to go down on me or something but instead when I looked up he was just tinkering with the crab thing in his hands.

'Almost there,' he said, winding what looked to be a key in the thing's back.

Then with a quiet interior clanking and whirring the thing started to move in his hands. On the ends of the four legs things like pincers opened and closed and the phallus in the middle drew itself up into the body of the thing.

'Lie down,' Icarus said, and I, being so obliging, did so.

The next thing I felt was the grip of cold metal on my thighs and round my ankles. I jumped but his hand on my belly held me down and I realised that the thing had a tight grip on my legs – two of its legs had gripped me on each side and when I peered down along my body I saw the little metal crabshell centred between my legs – its limbs spread out to steady it as it clung onto me.

'I'm going to set it going now,' Icarus said, as if he'd already explained the whole procedure to me, 'It might be uncomfortable at first, but I think you'll enjoy it.'

Before he did anything though the wise, smart, handsome lad stepped along the bench and kissed me on the lips, smoothed a strand of hair away from my eyes and, standing up, winked at me. Oh, the clever boy!

Then he vanished to the end of the workbench and clicked something on his little machine and slowly I felt something pressing at the little mouth between my legs. Of course I knew what it was, I have never been an idiot, and I remembered just how much bigger than Icarus' that new tool was.

But with the force of springs and cogs behind it and the naturally lubricious nature of that place, which was always ready to eat something when Icarus had led me off somewhere – it's like an instinctual response – the big member slowly slid in, stretching me and punishing me most wonderfully. I didn't worry, I didn't fear, because my boy was there and he had always built such marvellous toys. But as the thing kept heading further and further in – slowly, stately – I did wonder if it would stop before it came out the other end.

It did.

And then ever so slowly, just like before, it slid out. Ever such a slow, delightful, delicious slide out past my thickening lips – oh I'm sure they were blushing as much as they ever had, they were certainly weeping as much as they ever had... but, oh, it was heavenly. And then just as this mechanical manhood had slid almost all the way out, just an inch of it blocked my delightful doorway, I reckoned, it reversed direction and slid, ever so slowly back in again.

Oh, as I think about it now, it seems so mundane – just a machined tool slipping in and out of a hole. But it was magic it its own way. It was so different to being made love to by Icarus, for example, having this device strapped to me. I was entirely out of control. The boy I could tell 'Go faster... go slower... have a rest,' but he wasn't listening to me now and the machine was relentless in its slow thrusting, in and out, in and out. It was inorganic, it was mechanoid; it was without brain, without feeling, without compromise, without whims or desires of its own. All it knew was what it had been built to do, which was to hold on tight to something and to drive its column backwards and forwards. Whether I (or anything) was wrapped around it when it thrust forward was entirely of no consequence to it, it was without any care for such matters.

I was simply the tool of this tool and every time it drove all the way forward I was as full as I'd ever been, sweating and wriggling and giggling at the feeling; and every time it pulled all the way back, almost slipping out of my pouring little pouter, I was filled with breath and the fear that it was about to break, about to run out of energy and fail to thrust back in. Thank the gods it never did. Icarus kept it wound tight and as the hour went on he turned the handle and the thrusting increased in speed.

It was still regular, still relentless, still unstoppable, but it was quicker, faster, and more intense because of it. Oh, I was humming and blushing and laughing so much that I hardly paid any attention to the squelching, slurping and spitting noises that were filling the room. I'm embarrassed now to think of the sight that Icarus must have seen of that tool pounding in and out through the sodden curls around that dripping, spurting little mouth, but now I laugh and smile at the memory of it. All this that happened just a few months ago, but so far away and which will never be repeated. Gods, I'm so sad thinking of it.

There came a point when I thought I could take no more of this mechanical love-making, this wound-up pounding, but Icarus wouldn't listen to my requests to stop it, to switch it off, to let it wind down. I'd come again and again, forced over peak after peak by its unstoppable, unslowable, untireable thrusting and I was certain there was no more coming left in me – I was exhausted even if the machine was not.

'But wait,' he said, giving me his hand, 'The genius of this design – it's just a prototype you know – is that... well, stand up...'

As ever, I would do anything for the boy and he helped me to my feet. My legs were shaky, they certainly felt wonderfully weak, but the fact that they were wedged apart by the grip of the mechanical crab-toy helped them stay still. I could just about stand, and to my surprise the machine didn't fall. It remained just where it was as I lent against the workbench, still thrusting its great prong into exactly where it had been thrusting it all along. I laughed again, giggled, gripped the boy, lent my head on his shoulder as the spider-thing continued, entirely undistracted, to fuck me.

I came again, just like that. And again.

Eventually he let the spring of the thing wind down and

it slowed and finally stopped with its glorious fat member wedged high up inside the throat of my secret little mouth.

I stayed where I was, leant against the bench, and Icarus scrabbled between my legs, unhooked the tight metal pincers, which had dug, unnoticed, but painfully, into my thighs, leaving rich dark welts ('Ah,' he said, 'I should pad those,' and then he explained how he wanted to make the thing much smaller, so that a particularly excitable lady might wear such a device wherever she wanted – the crazy, dirty boy!), and then he slid the beautiful masculine thing out of me. With a pop and a dribble I was finally emptied.

The boy stood in front of me and licked my juices off of it, looking all the world as if he was an expert at mouthing a member. He had so many talents! I'd've liked to have seen that one in action just once. But oh! I felt so empty after having been so full for so long. I don't know how long that night had gone on for but he helped me back to my room and I slept until long into the day. It was glorious and sad and I cried in dreams that were disturbing and vague and which I've long since forgotten all detail of.

It was just a month or two later that my father, the king, caught us.

I was on my knees in Daedalus's workshop worshipping at Icarus' altar when he walked in. At first he laughed and complemented the boy on his good fortune, but when he looked closer and discovered, not some wench of the palace, but his daughter with her mouth full, he flew into the expected rage. It's always one rule for one and another the rest.

I was sent to my room, indefinitely, and Icarus was locked away under sentence of death. His father was to be banished, to be sent back to Athens, father said, a town he had been

exiled from so many years ago under threat of death. So, a death sentence for father and son and a life of ignoble imprisonment for me. That's how it looked.

From the balcony of my chamber I watched the Athenian ship arrive with the black sails, bringing the victims for the Minotaur and I hatched a plan. A rash, impetuous plan, but nonetheless a plan which, in some ways, actually seems to have worked. It got me as far as Naxos, more or less unscathed, and that has to count for something, doesn't it?

# vii.

I remember last night. I remember we'd beached the boat and the sailors had set the tents and started the fire and they roasted a goat they'd trapped in the hills for our dinner. I remember all that.

I was astounded that we had made it this far without being caught up with and caught. They said it was Naxos. And I knew that Naxos was far from Crete and that my father would never find me there. At least that's what I'd hoped.

We were all tired after having come so far so fast, but the Athenians were also eager to celebrate their victory and their survival. They pulled out instruments – a beautiful tortoiseshell lyre, some drums and pipes – and some of the women, so recently under sentence of death in the Minotaur's lair, danced in the flickering light of the camp fire. If I hadn't been sitting with Theseus and sharing his plate I might've got up myself, but these women knew different dances to any I'd seen back home in Crete and they all knew one another – I was just the strange girl who'd been picked up along the way. They didn't even look at me much. The men, however, paid me more attention. I think they were jealous that I was on Theseus's arm and not theirs.

But then in the middle of the dancing and feasting a cry came up from one of the sailors. He was outside the firelight and we couldn't see him, but all the men jumped to their feet when they heard it, dropping their instruments and stilling the evening air.

At first they thought he was being attacked or in trouble, but it turned out this fellow who'd gone off to relieve himself, had simply stumbled over a hidden cache of wine.

The men hurriedly dragged the heavy amphorae back into the camp and set about divulging each sealed flask of its contents. Even the women were encouraged to quaff and even I, the stray Cretan amongst these proud and haughty Greeks, was given more than a few cups of the heady brew. Oh, the singing and dancing recommenced and grew ever wilder and more astonishing. Dancing drummers and high-kicking pipers joined the girls as they twirled giddily around the fire and those men not too dozy to keep time clapped along and cheered and yelled every time someone performed an outstanding twirl, leap or stumble.

Theseus stood up, holding my hand and pulling me to my feet, and spun me into the midst of this mayhem.

I immediately found my feet as best I could, because it was a case of join in or be trampled by these mad-eyed dancers. I jigged around the circle, avoiding swinging arms and drums and cloaks, and I hopped into the air at the appropriate time and in short order I was quite swept up with the frenzy.

The drums were insistent and I sang along with the melodies of the pipes as they caught my ear and I swirled around and around, feeling ever more dizzy, but ever more merry too. I was sweating and panting and still I danced on. I couldn't... I wouldn't be seen to be the first to tire, to break ranks and have a sit down – I had something to prove to these Athenians, especially these Athenian girls who thought themselves so much better than me. (They hadn't said anything, but I could tell from the looks they gave me, underhand and sly and spiteful, and from the fact that they literally hadn't said anything to me – it was as if I didn't exist for them, except they were being constantly reminded that I actually did exist by seeing me clinging to the arm of their great prince – handsome, much-loved Theseus.)

But I couldn't keep this dancing up forever. I knew that, and my legs were aching, my chest was fighting to get enough air into it – oh, I was unable to outlast them, and I collapsed, out of the circle. Strong arms pulled me away from the skipping, dancing feet and as I passed out I knew I was safe.

Except, when I woke up again I suddenly realised I wasn't.

Exactly what had happened in the interim I'll never know, but Theseus seemed to have changed his mind about me.

I was tied up. My wrists were tied fast behind my back.

My shoulders pressed into the sand and under my bottom were pillows or cushions or stacked blankets, raising that part of me up in the air – up in the air and on display.

There was music still paying and the sound of the dance still clattered and laughed somewhere behind me.

There were hands on my shoulders, firm hands that held me tight, and there was something pushing its way between my legs.

I opened my eyes, I shouted out, but nothing changed. The world stayed the same and I was trapped in it.

Theseus himself was pinning me down as one of his sailors, an old man with a face scarred by decades of salt spray and wind, forced his way inside me. Looking around I could see the other Athenians watching and waiting; playing with their half-hard things as they queued up for their turn.

Struggle as I might, and I did, I was just a girl and no match, no challenge for these men. Theseus never bragged about his lineage but I'd heard who his father was, and though he shared that in common with my father's father, the blood had thinned somewhat by the time it reached me. I had no escape.

My screams and cries were swallowed in the night, submerged under the music that was playing, under the roar of the waves as the night-wind drove them up into a frenzy.

As one sailor finished in me, spitting his slime onto my belly or letting it drip out of my little mouth, another sailor would take his place, banging away in the wet hole, as Theseus laughed and spoke with them, encouraged them. I was just booty, a prize he wished to share, from insolent, vanquished Crete handed out free for these Athenians to use, as if I meant nothing to their prince, as if I hadn't made him love me after all.

Man after man burrowed his way into me that night and I resigned myself to it. As wretched and despicable as I felt I knew I couldn't escape, couldn't break free of them, and if I could where was there to run? There was nowhere. So I shut my eyes, thought of Icarus, who I'd adored in his own way, in my own way, and I repeated to myself how each one of these pathetic, soft-cocked, dumb as seamen, Athenians was a dreadful lover. Oh, I had variety that night for sure, as many men as any open-legged hot-holed woman might want in a lifetime; and I was done this way and that, turned over and taken the other way, and some of them did weird things I can barely remember; but what good is such wide choice of partners if they're all utter rubbish at it?

If I'd been Circe, oh they'd have lost their will soon enough. If she'd been there, that meddling, dangerous woman they'd've soon found their hopeless little things turned to snakes or to worms. I can see them now stood on the beach screaming as they touched these shrivelled little pieces, all shedding skin or spitting mud, mad with the thought that this is what it has all come to – a sly, quick, victory-slide and then a lifetime of explaining how this metamorphosis occurred to the wife who's waiting oh so patiently back home.

Oh, I'd've laughed so much at that. Just a bit of black magic in a miserable, panicked night. But, of course, I'm not Circe, and I don't know where she is, so the sailors just had their way again and again and eventually they grew tired and I, battered, leaking and sore as anything, sobbing, heartbroken, shattered to the core, was dumped on the sand, trussed like a sow for the slaughter, as they stumbled to bed, the wine finally catapulting itself into their heads.

That at least made me feel a little pride in amidst all the humiliation and pain: the fact they felt it necessary to tie me up while they slept, as if I might murder them all in their beds while they snored. I could've done that, I suppose, if I'd been more my father's daughter, but I'd never killed a man before and I didn't think I had what it would take to wield that knife, slipping it down into the tender neck, opening the artery there like breaking the wax seal on an upturned amphora. No, I couldn't do it, all the blood, all the gasping. The drowned fish look. But all the same it was nice to know these bastards on the beach were secretly afraid of me, simply because, for some years, my father had been slaughtering their youth. It's strange they couldn't tell the difference between him and me, or between the Minotaur and me.

Angry, weeping and resigned to the knots behind my back I finally passed out as dawn was stroking the far horizon. Even on this island I'd never been to before, birds were singing to welcome the sight, even here life and everything involved with it was going on – those little celebrations that nature throws, that dawn chorus, were recognised even here, so far from civilisation. How strange, I thought, slipping into a dark and dreamless sleep.

Eventually, in the full glare of day, I slowly woke, groggy and muddle-headed. I ache in every muscle, in each limb and in those places in-between. My hands had been untied while I slept and the miserable black-sailed ship has vanished from the beach. I don't even see it on the horizon, but I curse it all the same.

Last night feels like a dream, as if I can't be sure what happened, as if a variety of last nights happened and they all exist within me.

My head is killing me, pounding like a huge drum, slowly, but with great resonance.

And here I stand, almost alone on this lonely beach, clutching my head and confused about things.

# viii.

There was a time when I wasn't so confused, just a week ago.

I was locked in my room, and Icarus was locked in a cell under sentence of death. Gods I felt bad. I'd spent days crying long silent tears. I was sure I'd never see him again (I didn't) and I was equally sure I'd never get away from this dark palace with its secrets and its hate (I did).

From my balcony I watched Theseus' ship arrive. I knew it brought the tribute from Athens, the seven young men and the seven young women my father demanded each year to placate the Minotaur and his wrath. My brother, not the Minotaur, but the human one, had died at the games in Athens and my father blamed Aegeus, their king, personally. It was an accident that had turned out especially bad for Athens.

I saw the victims unloaded and as it was already late in the day I watched the ship tie up for the night. The sailors would be entertained as guests ought to be, while the others would languish in the holding cells outside the Labyrinth.

I'd been past those cells once or twice as I'd toyed with that maze downstairs, and this evening I sneaked out of my room, past my sleeping guard (you'd've thought Minos might've done a better job at keeping me safe, but no, that's my father for you), and down through the place right to them.

The cages were unguarded, but very securely locked and double-locked. No one liked guard duty there because before being thrust blindfolded into the Minotaur's lair, people tended to cry and weep and moan and make all sorts of noise or offer inducements and bribes and try to strike bargains, much more so than an ordinary prisoner biding his sentence or waiting to hear the severity of his fine or whipping.

I held my torch up to the bars and called for Theseus to come over. I'd heard his name whispered by my maid and I knew who he was, how he had come boasting to be the one to finally put an end to the monster and Minos's monstrous reparations. That sort of pride and swagger I thought I could use.

He came over, asked who I was, looked at me long and thoughtfully, with the self-assurance of a man of power, of a man who'd been told by his sleep-around mother that his father was Poseidon. There was something a little golden about him though, something that seemed to lend some truth to the rumour.

I looked up at him, a head taller than me, with the biggest eyes I could muster. I looked away, I blushed, I spoke softly.

'I saw you,' I said, 'When you stepped off the boat.'

'Ship,' he corrected.'

'...off the ship,' I continued, pretending to stammer at my mistake, but not quite hopelessly, just shyly, 'And I have been unable to stop thinking of you, my king.'

'Oh, I am but a prince, pretty girl, no king yet, nor for many years to come... but one day.'

I talked some more, inanities, though not stupidities. I touched his knuckles where he gripped the bar – just laid my hand across them and left it there for a minute as we spoke before pulling it away as if suddenly noticing the unexpected touch.

I could tell he was falling for the act, like a mouse that approaches closer and closer to the mousetrap, all the time suspecting it of being just what it is, but finding with each step that no spring snaps shut, no door falls behind him, and so he ventures to venture a step closer and another step closer, until finally it goes off, just as he always expected it would, and he has no escape.

I don't know what Theseus really thought was happening, whether he suspected some maid of the palace was seducing him or some lonely courtier's daughter had crept away for an attempted tryst with a condemned man, but after a while of talking about little things I finally let drop my name.

'Princess?' he asked, clearly surprised.

'Oh yes,' I said, 'And not just that, but imagine... a princess in love with a prince. What could be the odds of that happening? Love at first sight, my prince, my one.'

'Ah, but...' he said, clearly meaning that it was a shame that such love should pop into existence on the night before the very day he was to be fed to the ravenous merciless mythical beast in my father's dungeon.

Behind him I could see his fellow prisoners were watching, were listening to this conversation. What they thought of the doe-eyed, flighty, clearly slightly deranged, lovelorn girl attempting to seduce their leader I don't know. I got the feeling from the way they shuffled their feet that they didn't think too much of it.

'Ah, but...' I repeated back at him, 'It's nothing. I can help you with that. The Labyrinth? The Minotaur? I have a key that takes me straight to him. I can get you a knife if that would be of help?'

Theseus stared wide-eyed at me. His mouth fell open in a most funny way – him, son of the gods and prince of his people, dumb-founded by a little girl. I smiled demurely and laid out my terms.

'My lord, my prince, my love. All I ask is that you take me with you. If my father discovers I have helped you, then my life will be forfeit. Let me come by your side and together we can help heal the rift between our two countries. Imagine that, the prince and princess of our two overly proud nations, in love together...'

For a moment he seemed to think, as if this was an offer any man would have to think about, and then he agreed.

'Princess Ariadne, I am yours to command,' he said, just the words I'd wanted to hear.

He put his face up to the bars, obviously feeling that now we had plighted some sort of troth he ought to, or maybe wanted to (and after all, I'm young and pretty, so who wouldn't?), seal the deal with a kiss.

I brushed my lips over his as they protruded between the cold metal poles, and it was pleasant enough, but just to really set the seal on things and to ensure I wasn't left behind at the first opportunity, I wanted to prove myself really indispensable, to really win his love. So I lowered myself to my knees and reached through the bars.

I didn't see the look on his face as I reached under his tunic, but I can imagine it. He was really something of a prude I think, though that didn't stop him from standing up when I applied my ministrations.

With a firm grip I pulled him to the bars, and lifted his tunic. Underneath he had a most handsome member, all fat and hot in my little hand and with a dark smooth head poking out of its little covering.

It was wider than Icarus's, but not as novel. I decided right away, however lovely it was (and the way it throbbed in my hand and the solid feel of it as I slipped it between my lips were really rather lovely ndeed) that it wasn't as good as my boy's had been and it made me sad to think I'd never see it again.

I'd so loved to do things with Icarus. At the time I'd thought we were just playing about, that he held this secret over me that I couldn't bear for him to tell anyone about (about my mother and my half-brother and all that) and so I let him do things to me, and then it turned out that I was letting him do things with me, because I was bored and I was lonely and I hadn't realised how lonely I had been. And then we were doing things with each other, a balance was reached and he'd let me take charge sometimes and I'd worry about him at night and in time it turned out we weren't just messing about, weren't just having a secret fling. Gods, I missed the boy and it had only been a few days, but I knew my father would keep his word and in a few days more he'd be dead.

There was no way get to his cell, no way to visit him even. There was no easy path to a key, no simple way to bribe the guards. My father was omnipotent in some areas of the palace and I was without power at all. But sometimes a princess has to be ruthless, has to be selfish, has to think of herself, to put herself first and I knew – or at least I told myself that I knew – that my boy would have wanted me to get away, to escape, to make for the hills. This wasn't the sort of love that demanded a suicide pact, but all the same I swear I did love that boy.

Poor Icarus, poor me. How could anyone expect me to stay in a house where, against the odds and against all expectations I had finally been happy? How could I stay when my one spark of fire, my beam of sunshine, my genius, my love, my enthusiasm was murdered? I had to go.

I slipped as much of Theseus into my mouth as I could, sucked hard on him, refused to let him out of there until the vacuum was as total as I could make it, then I let him slide slowly, grazing the length of him with my teeth, smoothing and snaking round him with my tongue, and then I repeated the action. Time and again.

Theseus groaned ever so quietly above me and I heard some chuckles and some tutting from his companions. I smiled to think they were seeing their leader undone, even so pleasantly, because at the end of the day all leaders, all princes and kings are too high up and need to be levelled. And oh, I was going to level Minos all right.

With that thought I sucked harder. I took hold of the length of him that extended through the bars and manhandled it, pulling it up and down, watching the loose layer of skin running across the fixed ridges and vessels within, knocking my fingers across the sudden edge of the head of the thing, banging again and again, bringing him further and further under my power. Oh, how could a man resist such a thing like this? I'd watched Icarus swoon from the repetition, that boy who was so virile, so hot for me, he'd shut his eyes and muttered about the impossible plans he was making – I was inspiring, he said, I set ideas hurtling through his head, but too fast, he claimed, always they went too fast and he could never grab hold of them. Ah, but the things he saw, the possibilities he knew were out there if only he could one day pin them down, sketch them, but oh! And then he would come, squirting his egg-white seed into the air like a fountain, jet after jet. And in my hand his descending member would jerk of its own accord, trying to propel the last few hot teardrops into the air and failing. They'd creep out of the end, latecomers, gatecrashers weeping slowly out of that jolly little eye and I'd lick them off him, as sour and unpleasant as they were.

Oh, my happy boy. And as I tugged at Theseus I imagined the same thing would happen, but he stopped me short, muttering something about the Minotaur, something about his friends, something about how fast dawn approaches.

I let him go, let him tuck himself away, but I think I had convinced him of my honesty and of my worth. Even if I hadn't convinced him of my love, or convinced him of his love for me, at least I may have convinced him that I wasn't just some trick sent by my father. What father would make his daughter do something like that?

I'd brought the key from the guardhouse and used it to unlock the cage. Theseus sent his fellows down to the docks, to rouse the sailors and to ready the ship. He and I, on the other hand, headed the other way, into the mouth of the labyrinth. If they fled and the Minotaur lived then there would be more sacrifices next year. This had to end now, and I was quite happy to see that hideous insult of a brother of mine ended too.

We followed my mother's secret straight way, closing the doors after us and tip-toeing as if we might be heard, and we found ourselves stood outside the central chamber, the bed-chamber. My brother was asleep, we could hear him snoring like a thunderstorm. Theseus crept in, with the knife in his hand, and slit the monster's throat.

It didn't even wake up. It just gurgled and gurgled wetly until finally there was silence.

Then we fled.

# ix.

We fled to this island, Naxos, and now I've been left behind in my turn.

As my head pounds and the sun shines far too brightly, I run the soft white sand through my toes. At least something is soft, something is harmless. I'm sat on the head of the beach looking down at where the camp was last night. I can see indentations in the sand, a scorched circle where the fire was, the odd bit of detritus left behind (with me) by those thoughtless Greeks. But when I think about last night, about the last few days everything is hazy.

It's as if, when I try to concentrate my head splits into two or three or four different instances of 'me'; it's as if cause and effect isn't as simple as in actual fact it is. I suspect it is just a symptom of this hangover, although a part of me remembers not drinking anything last night. Oh, the world is a strange and awkward place.

And now I'm no longer alone. There on the dune to my right is a figure, silhouetted by the sun. I can't quite make him out, even as I squint and cover the sun with my hand, he remains difficult to see. But he walks towards me and with a start I realise that I saw him last night. On a last night at any rate.

'Good morning,' he says, sitting down beside me.

'Good morning,' I answer.

We sit for a while in silence, just listening to the slow splash and suck of the waves and lazy calling of the gulls as they wheel around looking for breakfast.

I half-watch this man from the corner of my eye. I try to be subtle about these things.

Perhaps he's middle-aged, though it's hard to tell. He seems impossible to pin down, not for cosmetic reasons, but simply because the idea of him seems to always evade capture, to avoid any simple definition. It's hard to explain. If I turn to look at him he remains still, his face is one face, his beard is one beard and his eyes are one colour, but if I look away and look back he seems to have changed all round, even though his face and his beard and his eyes are just the same. There's something slippery about the memory of him. But it's not worrying, not disconcerting, because he seems so lazy, so warm, so genuine.

His cloak is a deep, rich purple – an astonishing thing. And his irises are a much paler shade of the same colour – not quite so obvious as to be freakish, but quite clear enough to not be a trick of the light.

He holds his hands up to the air as if reaching for something, though there is nothing there, and for a moment he seems to fumble, as if fiddling with something tricky. It's an intriguing, amusing little mime and I watch closely and I do not see the moment when he produces the fruit from his sleeve, though I assume, for a moment, that that is what has just happened.

'A grape?' he asks, holding the dark little sphere between finger and thumb.

'Yes, it is' I reply.

His young eyes narrow and then he smiles.

'No, what I meant was 'would you like...' oh.' He stops talking as I take the sweet sphere from between his fingers and pop it into my mouth.

And, oh!, it's good. Now I smile as the juice saturates my mouth, turns my tongue purple, trickles like nectar down my dry and tasteless throat.

'Ariadne?' he asks.

'Yes, it is,' I reply.

His eyes narrow again and again he smiles.

His smile is like a balm. Each time I see it another dull throb and creaking piece of machinery in my head eases. If he keeps on like this my hangover will be gone in just another minute or two.

'Um, Ariadne,' he says again, 'Where is your father? I'd like to ask him something.'

'My father,' I answer slowly. The day grows dim again, clouds sweep in from the north and the sun vanishes behind them.

'Yes, I need to make a deal with him.' He hiccoughs and scratches at his beard.

I think for a moment, run my toes through the sand.

I think of my poor Icarus and I think of the different evenings I remember living through last night. They all seem like dreams, but there's something entirely undreamlike about them all – none of them are fading away from me, though all of them have their hazy moments. But somehow they are all staying with me, in exactly the way dreams don't. And one of those nights involved this man sat next to me, I'm sure of it. And I think of Icarus again and my heart breaks with fear.

'My father is dead,' I say, feeling quite sure about stating such an untrue thing. He's dead to me.

'Oh, is there someone else I should talk to?'

'Why?'

'I, well, this is a bit embarrassing...'

I sit quietly looking at the waves and wait for him to go on.

He doesn't, at least not for a good while.

He looks at me though. I don't turn to him, but I can feel his eyes following the contours of my face, and it's almost as if he's touching me. Those pale violet eyes are tracing me out, like an artist might first sketch down the outlines of his model, as a poet might first weigh a few images, metaphors and rhymes in his mind before starting in to sing them. This stranger was interested in me in a way few people have been.

I'm aware of this going on, somehow, but demurely I keep my eyes on the sea, on the rolling waves.

They are a deep, transparent blue and they have stopped. In mid wave, with white foam flecking along the dipping crest, they have stopped, as if the whole world has stopped. Except it hasn't because I lift my hand up and that moves freely through the air.

I look around me. High up to my left a seagull perches motionless, wings spread wide, in the air. Clouds are stopped, too. There is a silence here quite unlike any I've heard before.

I turn to the stranger sat beside me. He fiddles with his hands in front of him, as if he should be nervous. It's just me and him alive and awake and aware in this moment, I know this. He has stopped the world so that he can have this conversation. And now he's not even having the conversation. I find that quite sweet, if, likely, a little infuriating in the long run.

I know as well as I know anything that mortal men can't stop the world. I'm sure even god-sired Theseus wouldn't be able to stop the world at a clap of his hands.

As I look at the stranger he seems to shift uncomfortably at the edge of my perception. It's as if he is a protean panoply of different animals, of men, of ideas. It's so hard to understand just what I'm seeing, especially since all the time he remains just a man.

And I realise with the absolute certainty of truth that I'm being propositioned by a god. He wants to offer a marriage gift to my father in exchange for me, because that's the mortal way of doing things and he's trying so hard to fit in with what he thinks I might expect. How sweet. But my father has killed the only man I could love and he deserves no more respect from me, nor from this god. My father has only ever disrespected the gods and from that beginning all the curses of Crete have come.

This stranger sat beside me is the crux of a hundred different potential worlds, more so than any other god in the pantheon – I can feel the choices emanating from him, like sweat from a bull's back, he is multifarious and marvellous. Every life lived with him, I suddenly know, will be a life lived a hundred different ways, with all possibilities explored, with all the roads less taken, taken. I'm filled with the supernatural knowledge of this (and many other things), as if I knew all along.

I'm on a beach hundreds of miles from a home I can't return to, hundreds of miles from the city I thought I was going to, but with no way of getting there now and no likelihood of a friendly welcome. I could starve on this beach, on this little island perhaps, or maybe I'd find food, find shelter and eke out a prideless shipwrecked existence all by myself.

I can't help but think of Icarus and I know what he would want me to do (I certainly know what he would do were the tables the other way round and he found this unspoken offer being made to him). 'Go on,' he'd say, 'Take the adventure; start the new experiment...' I wish he could've been here with me, but he's not. It's just me and this stranger who has a way with metamorphoses, who has a talent for the vine, who is stranger than anyone I have ever met.

I'm not a girl given to him, not in the traditional sense, but I am a girl who is open to the idea of apotheosis and who is getting hungrier by the minute.

A flicker from the corner of my eye sees the world fall back into motion.

'Would you like another grape... look,' he says as he plucks a beautiful plump one from nothing but the air.

He passes it to me and I pop it in my mouth, feel the skin break against my tongue, savour the little slit that opens, flick the cold flesh inside. I crush it to pulp on the roof of my mouth, swallow it down without chewing, let the juice soak through me, all the way through me, finally, fully waking me up.

'Thank you,' I say.

*Endnote*

It might be suggested that not all of the happenings in this book are, in the strictest sense of the term, canonical. And, of course, whoever suggests such a thing is, in the strictest sense, absolutely correct. But all tellings of these stories are retellings, and that is as true for Hesiod, Homer and Ovid as it is for Graves, Logue and Crossley-Holland. Retellings produced for Erotic Review Books have a natural exaggeration of flavour in one particular direction, but there is very little in this book that is not simply an expansion on the versions recorded by earlier writers.

For those who care about these things, what is unrecorded in the canon is the chapter in Zeus In Love entitled Now: One which is an imagined example taken from the many rumoured 'seductions' of mortal women by the god, but purposefully avoiding any of the well-known cases which usually feature metamorphoses of one sort or another. The author thought a straightforward romp might be the simplest way to start him off. Otherwise everything that Zeus does (to Ganymede, Danaë, Callisto and with Semele) has some basis (details aside) in the generally agreed versions of the stories.

In Pasiphaë Speaks the broad outline is as agreed by most ancient sources (Diodorus Siculus, for example, says (IV.77.1) 'Now according to the myth which has been handed down to us Pasiphaë, the wife of Minos, became enamoured of the bull, and Daedalus, by fashioning a contrivance in the shape of a cow, assisted Pasiphaë to gratify her passion'), though some of the specific details and incidents have been expanded. As far as the author can discover there is, however, no classical suggestion that she had any interaction with the Minotaur once it was interred in the labyrinth. The inspiration for imagining there may have been came from a series of drawings by Picasso drawings which featured the Minotaur sleeping on a bed while being watched from behind a curtain by some unspecified woman; the story unpacked itself from that starting point.

In Ariadne Speaks the uncanonical aspect is, of course, her relationship with Icarus. The only explanation for that is the author felt sure she had some sort of life before Theseus and Dionysus sweep into it, and Icarus was the young man in the palace at Knossos who would likely have had, not only the chutzpah, but also the opportunity to romance her.

Facts established in Pasiphaë's monologue eliminate the need for the legendary ball of string that Theseus used at Ariadne's suggestion to navigate the labyrinth; and Minos' discovery of Icarus and Ariadne together is banal enough (and likely enough) a reason for the boy's death for mythographers (such as, perhaps, Daedalus on his arrival back in Attica) to invent some more interesting story.

As for Ariadne's manifold experience on Naxos, this is explained in either one of two ways (or both, if you're feeling expansive): firstly, the nature of Dionysus is distinctly metamorphic and protean – much like the cumulative effect of the wine he is responsible for – possibilities expand whenever he is around, and sometimes it can be hard to remember in the morning exactly which story is true. Secondly, and more prosaically, Ariadne's desertion on Naxos and subsequent marriage to Dionysus is a story that has very many recorded variants.

Plutarch writes in his Life Of Theseus (XX): 'There are many other stories about these matters [Theseus' flight from Crete], and also about Ariadne, but they do not agree at all.'

What is true and simple is that Dionysus, who makes his appearance on the beach at Naxos, is the same child that Zeus saves from the destruction of Semele. He rescues the embryo, sews it into his thigh and when the time is right gives birth to the child, who from then on leads a most fraught and bizarre life as an immortal wandering all over the earth, turning all sorts of things and people into all sorts of other things, and spreading the vine around the classical world.

The narrators of these short stories are naïve of many things – Zeus, for example, is clearly not aware quite how much his behaviour actually does irk Hera, his dynastic wife. According to Apollodorus, for example, (The Library, III.iv.3) 'But Zeus loved Semele and bedded her unknown to Hera. Now Zeus agreed to do for her whatever she asked, and deceived by Hera she asked that he would come to her as he came when he was wooing Hera.'

Finally, Zeus, being immortal and a god, knows of all sorts of things outside the narrow timespan he is usually associated with, thus his quoting of 18th and 19th century poets, and any anachronistic use of language (any talk of electricity, for example, or gravity or a knowledge of synapses or of the circulation of the blood) is purely intentional. However, any similar anachronisms that occur in the other two monologues (both by, more or less, mortal women) are purely the result of the author's over-hasty carelessness.

AFH, Reading, June 2007.

# Some more titles available from the ER Books:

## The Diary of a Sex Fiend     £9.99

### Christopher Peachment

If you're a serious subscriber to political correctness, then this book is probably not for you. But if you are a genial, intelligent and well balanced Renaissance man or woman (as most of us are), then you can do no better than to order this book. In return you will receive a vast repository of acerbic wit, sharp wisdom and an astonishing amount of pithy sexual fact written by the Erotic Review's top columnist, Christopher Peachment.

## Rogering Molly & other stories     £7.95

### Christopher Hart

From the small market towns of mid-Wales to the narrow streets of ancient Babylon, from a lofty Singapore penthouse (with a rooftop pool the size of Surrey) to a woodland shack deep in the forests of Transylvania, the sexual predators are afoot, and... they're hungry. With an extensive cast of wickedly erotic characters, Hart shows himself to be a subtle master of the genre in these 25 lubricious tales.

## The Main Point     £7.95

### Bruno Philips

The story of Bernd Töst and his career as a porn-movie auteur is as colourful and strange as any in the history of pornography. Gathering together stories from the stars of his films, his family, and the great man himself, Töst's erotic biography is the most fascinating expose of the early porn industry and its players since *Boogie Nights*.

## Dirty Habits and Other Stories     £7.95

### John Gibb

From fairy tales and fighter jets to religion and royalty, John Gibb uncovers erotic potential at every turn in this brilliant collection of 30 tales. He is able to manipulate the most innocent elements of everyday life and turn them into passionate moments imbued with sensual power. Every tale is intriguing, surprising, and completely different form those that have gone before. Some are dark and tense, some quirky and humorous, but none will disappoint in their ability to arouse and excite.

Orderline: 0800 0262 524

Email: leadline@eroticprints.org

# WWW.EROTICPRINTS.ORG

Please contact us for a catalogue